Praise for Bacon's work

MAGE OF FOOLS
"*Mage of Fool*'s lush narrative, vivid characterization and expertly constructed world help signify why Eugen Bacon is one of the most talented writers working in speculative fiction today."— Professor John Jennings, NYTimes Bestselling author, and graphic novelist. Hugo-award winner for *Parable of the Sower: A Graphic Novel Adaptation*.

DANGED BLACK THING
"Eugen Bacon is an exhilarating writer. Her work is daring, fierce, visceral and sensual, fast paced and packed with action, earthed yet given to flights of fancy. It is driven by empathy for the eccentric and marginalised, a simmering anger at injustice and inequality, and a deep concern for the big questions..."—Arnold Zable

ROAD TO WOOP WOOP
"Bacon is at her best when spinning yarns of fantastic creatures and otherworldly beings, many of which derive from African or Australian traditions."—*BSFA Review*

CLAIMING T-MO
"Bacon's whole book feels itself like a fairytale, albeit one where mystical planets and traveling between stars take the place of castles and sorcery. That said, there is a peculiar witchcraft at work... It resembles the writing of N.K. Jemisin, particularly in the way it nests the human in the fantastic, and it incorporates the kind of galaxy-spanning scope of generations once used by Octavia E. Butler."—NPR

WRITING SPECULATIVE FICTION
"Bacon encourages us as readers and writ
differently, to expand our normative way
humanity through the wonder of speculat
fantastical, horrifying, and edifying 'what

Published by Raw Dog Screaming Press
Bowie, MD
First Edition

Book design: Jennifer Barnes
Cover art: Lynne Hansen
LynneHansenArt.com

Printed in the United States of America
ISBN: 978-1-947879-44-7

Library of Congress Control Number:
2022938505

www.RawDogScreaming.com

CHASING WHISPERS

Eugen Bacon

**RAW DOG
SCREAMING
PRESS**

Publisher's Note

Because Bacon is an African Australian writer we have chosen to retain the spelling conventions that are the standard in Australia.

Contents

Dedication

To
The Katharine Susannah Prichard Writers' Centre
&
The Swan Valley in the upper reaches of the Swan River in Western
Australia
for
Provoking my stories.

~~~

To
Jennifer Barnes
&
Raw Dog Screaming Press
for
Unquestioning my stories.

Towards an Afro-Irreality

D. Harlan Wilson

When I first read Eugen Bacon's *Chasing Whispers*, I was at once estranged by the writing and familiar with it. The stories in this collection felt like they belonged in my head even as they escaped me. I remember texting the editor and saying: "I like this book! It reminds me of ... me?"

Granted, I have a love-hate relationship with my own writing, and I never read a book of my own once I've finished it: all I see are the imperfections, the deficiencies, the unborn ideas and underdeveloped strophes. The same goes for most twenty-first-century fiction. I don't like it. Almost everything I see is what I've seen before, so I turn to previous centuries, where authors not only valued genuine innovation but made concerted efforts to be original and new. In the nineteenth and twentieth centuries, I see so much writing that challenges me to be an active rather than a passive reader—intellectually and imaginatively, it forces me to engage with the material, whereas contemporary fiction just washes over me like lukewarm bathwater.

This is an illusion, of course. Certainly there are working authors who continue to push boundaries and defy conventions even as we become less literate, less perceptive, and more unplugged from history, regardless of the chronic informational deluge fed to us on a daily basis from the motherbird of our screens. We live in a science fictional world distinguished by a terroristic Superfluity. Everybody is a *de facto* Talking Head and a Dancing Marionette, and self-awareness is a fairytale. As for literature, the digital age has relieved the medium of its momentum. The literary novel, for instance, used to be a beacon of culture. Now it's a special-interest venture at best.

Some people get upset when I disparage the state of art, literature, and culture at large, but I can't help myself. The Image has usurped the flows of our desires and (un)consciousness, relegating the Word to a necessary evil. We don't remember how to read. *Moby-Dick* might as well have been written by an alien from another dimension: the depth of Melville's allusions alone is entirely lost on twenty-first century generations. Likewise, *Ulysses* had trouble getting published 100 years ago in 1922. It's totally unpublishable today. If nobody knew who Joyce was, even a small press wouldn't touch it. Too long; too complex. Above all: too artistic, creative, and intelligent.

Melville and Joyce are two of the most recognizable figures in the modern literary canon. They're also two of the whitest figures.

The further we go back in literary history, the whiter it gets. Thankfully, times are a-changin' once again. Not fast enough—worthwhile movements rarely move fast enough—but we're finally starting to march ahead. We need more diversity in our literature. We need to recognize more underrepresented voices, namely authors of color. But that doesn't mean we should turn our backs on canonical authors. The most accomplished writers (and readers) familiarize themselves with the megatext of art and literature and culture at large. Buried in the garden of the megatext are the seeds of our own identities, and the best versions of ourselves emerge from a well-roundedness of thought and experience. That said, *Ulysses* and *Moby-Dick* are vast exercises in ennui. Stupidly, I've taught both of these novels in undergraduate college courses, and I'll never do it again: the incomprehension, boredom, and anger they incited in my students reflected my own feelings for my students' textual intolerance and helplessness. But Joyce and Melville are writer's writers who foreground style as a way of seeing. For my part, I don't "enjoy" reading *Ulysses* and *Moby-Dick*. I can't stand *Ulysses*, in fact. But goddamn it if Joyce didn't weaponize his imagination.

This is exactly what I think of my own fiction in terms of aspiring for originality and the Poundian incentive to Make It New. You may not like what I write—I don't even like it, half the time—but goddamn it if I'm not trying hard to be consistently innovative. I'm not saying I'm Zarathustra; far from it. What I'm saying is that I don't see many authors trying to Make It New.

There's this idea that stories and novels must be written a certain way in order to be "good," and if they're not written that way, they're "bad." Throw a dart at a bookstore and I guarantee you'll hit a "good" book written by somebody who knows the Rules. Most M.F.A. programs, masterclasses, and writing textbooks will provide you with the same Rules. The Rules are important. The Rules must be learned and followed. Failure to learn and follow the Rules will result in a no-"good" book and, in most cases, a rejection from the publisher. In short, the Rules are the Rules—mind them or go do something else.

Eugen Bacon is an exception to the Rules. And contemporary literature needs more exceptions.

Broadly speaking, the stories in *Chasing Whispers* are picturesque explorations of minds and bodies that dabble in multiple genres. Foremost among these genres is irrealism. This is what caught my eye when I initially read the book. Irreal narratives combine dreamlike episodes or moments with an absurdist undercurrent in such a way that readers are at once estranged by the writing and familiar with it—which, as I noted in my first sentence, was *precisely* my experience. But so what? Why estrange readers? Why alienate them in any way? Readers don't like to be alienated. For the most part, they don't want to do any extra work. Our external screens imagine everything for us, showing us the payload in great detail. When we read, we have to show ourselves the payload on our internal screens, making images and sounds in our heads from words alone. Readers want this process to be as easy as possible. If people read at all, they want their words spoon-fed to them, with no nonsense or ambiguity. I understand that impulse. But that's not reality. Daily life is a torrent of nonsense and ambiguity. Listen to the news. Dissect last night's dreams. Think about the finality of death. Talk to an uneducated American. Look at the sky and try to fathom the universe's 200 billion trillion stars. There are more questions than answers, more absurdities than certainties, more untold desires than recycled actions and articulations.

Ironically, perhaps, irreal stories have the ability to depict "reality" better than "reality" itself because they can account for conscious and unconscious realms simultaneously, imploding objectivity and subjectivity. An effective work of irrealism, in other words, can come closer to representing how one might perceive the "real" world than a work of "realism." And perception is all that matters; without it, there is no one, no works, no world, no nothing. Everything we see—including our reflections in the mirror and in our dreams—should always be enclosed in quotes, because it's all bullshit. Only our capacity to see and interpret something makes something into something.

Irrealism is a thing in itself, but it's also a methodology wherein authors might express themselves and explore motifs intimate to their purview and personal history. Kafka is the touchstone—the epitome of the form, as I see it. His variety of irreal fiction thematized the absurdity of bureaucracy and portrayed the many ways in which he felt trapped by institutional antagonists (ranging from his father and family to his job, the Culture Industry, and even his body). Bacon's variety is an exploration of her experience as a black woman in a volatile, often menacing world whose default stance is objectification, racism, misogyny, patriarchy, heteronormativity ... In spite of recent movements such as Me Too and Black Lives Matter, this remains the default stance of the "real" world, and if history teaches us anything about the Human Stain, it will continue to be the norm for a long time.

Bacon draws on science fiction and fantasy as well as irrealism. Many of her decidedly Afro-Futuristic stories reminisce the fiction of Nisi Shawl, Nalo Hopkinson, Sheree Renée Thomas, and two of the modern literature's most important figures, Octavia Butler and Toni Morrison. Morrison's work has often been associated with magic realism, but technically that's a regional form that originated in Latin America and has been most effectively rendered by Gabriel García Márquez. To my mind, novels like *Beloved, The Bluest Eye*, and *Song of Solomon* exhibit elements of irrealism, which has no cultural ties.

Whatever the case, *Chasing Whispers* comfortably situates itself within the tradition of these authors. At the same time, Bacon's voice is unique—these stories have something new and different to say, and they're deeply informed by her life as an African Australian outsider who has, among other things, clearly endured the entitled assholery of Little Men. The violence, suffering, and anguish that marks the history of civilization is an invariable product of this assholery, and Bacon illustrates it with as much beauty as truth. In so doing, she enacts the title of this introduction, moving us towards an Afro-Irreality that calls attention to the haunted houses of the past, signals a better future, and accomplishes the increasingly rare feat of Making It New.

Literature has been dying the death for at least half a century now. Authors like Eugen Bacon are the life-support orgones that keep it alive.

Chasing Whispers

TODAY the house wore Zeda. She felt stretched. Necks and elbows tucked into her shawl. Fridges too. She was suffocating, and the house's monsters were responsible. Protrusions everywhere: belly buttons, kneecaps, pots, toilets.

At her worst point she was a blindfold, an ill-fitting ski mask over the patio. That was before she turned into a clown costume full of circus in the garage. Worse: the house was shedding sawdust and it stank—no deodorant could fix it. Vacuuming was useless.

It was as if the house was spiteful about something. She tried to cheer it up, smiled and twisted so it could fit better inside her shape. But the house grew more necks and corners. Bones, teeth and microwaves into her leotard.

She knew it wasn't the house. It was him. *Pepo.*

Touch is an open window and a door ajar. It's a familiar mall, the face of the future. Touch is fire, water, earth and air. It's a garden full of reflections and dreams. It's an archetype or a metaphor, or alchemy. It reminds you of a river or a beach, rain or sunshine. Touch is right here—you've arrived. The press of fingers tells you everything.

Everything.

And it's simultaneous, marvellous and not enough. You think of it again and again, ask what more you want and you cannot say. You don't linger on it because you're not crazy. Because touch may be an esplanade, but it's not insurance.

She remembers his online profile: EpsomSalts.

She imagined a soaker, a soother. A calmer. A rejuvenator. Her life was in shambles—aches and sprains, sore muscles everywhere. She wanted *EpsomSalts*. And he was right there, crisp on her screen. The laser focus of his eyes talked to her, only to her. What she felt was not whimsy, but a rush full of edge. He abducted her soul across a screen. She swiped right, even knowing how she always sacrificed in pursuit of love.

She messaged him first. She told him she powerwalked and jogged around trails. She said it was the first crack she'd given this kind of dating. "I don't know what I'm signing up for."

"Why not?" he said.

"Online's not my thing."

"What's a thing?"

She didn't know what to answer because, truth was, she didn't have a thing. She was relieved when he immediately asked to be exclusive, to take their 'discovery offline'—his very words.

"Yeah, maybe," Zeda said.

"It's an ending."

"What do you mean?"

"You don't need here," he said.

"Like online? But... I need to know you more. Before..."

"What will we say on chat that you can't see in person?"

"And that's better?" she asked.

He went silent three days, four hours and thirty-six seconds. She'd given up on him, was contemplating swiping right on another hunk, *AwesomeTriple6,* when Pepo resurfaced.

"It's molecular affinity—you and me both. Sunday. 10.30am. Meet at your house."

"You don't know where I live."

"That's why you'll tell me."

She did.

Their physical reaction to each other was spontaneous. Binding. Something crystallised. A release of energy in the compound of their copulating selves. It informed the thermodynamics of their relationship.

Every morn she woke up sapped, as if overnight he'd siphoned her energy. He was all bouncy. Laser eyes hypnotic.

She puts herself in the bath. Fills it with water, more hot than cold. She doesn't touch the soap. Doesn't touch the water. Not with her fingers, no. Just watches it rise, to her stomach, to her knees, her nose. She nearly lets it swallow her head, flood it with calm. A wail is swelling. It'll explode like a bomb.

She stays silent.

An ogre lurked inside those onyx eyes and platinum teeth. He reeked worse than a sewer. It got progressively worse each passing day, as though suppressant magic was waning. When did her knowing start?

Did she grow wary when he walked into the living room and a spurt of perfume sprinkled on a carcass hit Zeda's nose? Was it when he smiled across the table at dinner under candlelight chandeliers one night, and a bruise of green moss snailed from the corners of his closing mouth? Perhaps it was when they were walking in the park that autumn, past the gate and its sign that announced new closing times. There was a sweet scent of crushed fruit, golden leaves underfoot. But she wished for spring. She longed for the limy smell of freshly mowed grass. The velvety green of brand new leaves. It happened without warning: Pepo's chest pushed away from his body, as if escaping his hips. She didn't know how to feel, as he hunched, hobbled and shuffled all the way home.

That night sleep abandoned her. She opened her eyes to an intolerable pong, and saw the melt of Pepo's face right there on her bed, bubbling, blubbering, an ooze of bile.

She doesn't know how she slept, but she finally did. She woke to the noise of her neighbour's building works. Now a jack hammer, now a drill... She was frightened to get up. To pick up her phone and call in sick at work—for that is what she felt: sick. The walls of her world loosened, and imprisoned. Hell entered the hollow in her gut.

Pepo didn't speak a word. Nothing decipherable anyways. Just whispers she couldn't make out. Nor was she sure they came from him. He gobbled her terror, became more disjoined. Sometimes he was a shapeless whorl—still reeking, always whispering—swirling about the house. Obscure to her trauma. When his face fell, it was never in afterthought. It was deliberate, the way his nose melted and ran down his chin.

One day he looked at her in a way that said he knew that she knew.

She turns off the faucet. And when she speaks, it's two words in a voice of infinity in a torrent of seas and a destination she doesn't know.

"Yes. Mother."

After her father left, pieces of her childhood came and went.

Today she remembers when she was five. Her bladder was a balloon swollen with water, near leaking. She burst into the bathroom and stopped. He sat there, naked, her father. Baba. His gaze, at first startled, then swelled with adoration—like she was his most favourite. The sound from his throat reminded her of the mewl of a kitten. She remembered the fur. It was everywhere. It slimed down his face, slopped into the tub, and the water gurgled. It overflowed, clumps of it sodden on the floor, mingled with her panic and shame. It was her mother who lifted her from the sludge of sopping fur and her own pee.

Later she heard voices. Bellows, then whispers.

It was her father's neck, and his face—as if stretched from elsewhere—at the door of her bedroom, a deep and terrible sadness in his eyes.

That's all she remembers of him now.

Days after he was gone she wondered if he'd had a stroke and Mum secretly buried him in the backyard.

Zeda remembered Joel at work. How he purred one day, and she looked over the partition, and his head was a blob. She looked again and he was a hairless bird full of clots holding a sewer. She minded that. And his star-nose face, bulging eyes and sabre-tooth. How was it no-one else noticed?

She hadn't spoken to her mother in... what? She couldn't remember. Memory failed, since her father. Even more since meeting Pepo. Yet she lifted the phone and dialled without looking up contacts.

"Mum?"

"This a surprise, innit? All these years. What you want?"

"Mum. What happened to Baba?" She doesn't know why these first words after all that time.

"What Baba?"

The silence between them...

And then her mother, a stranger on the line, said, "The separation tree. Find it."

"The what?"

"It's everywhere. You just have to find it, don't ya?"

"Yes. Mother."

And godawful nothingness overwhelmed the phone.

The whispers are a brush of bottles and blurs, keys and tingles gathering speed around her ears. They rub against her skin, rotten camel hair imprinting bile-green images and afterimages of recursive disbelief in the shape of intestines. It's hard to tell why the sludge of black mud is streaming behind her eyes, so she lies to herself that it's a dimension, as the water goes cold.

A separation tree? She looked it up online, found there was a huge and ancient river red gum now dead in the Royal Botanical Gardens. It had a historic significance in 1850 to celebrate Victoria's separation as a colony from New South Wales. She read about vandals, ringbarking a 400-year-old tree... News articles went on and on about the loping, sculpting and final plaquing of the age-old red gum. Web page after page *1 2 3 4 5 6 > Next...*

At last she found text burrowed like a secret, halfway down the eleventh page of online search results:

A <u>separation tree</u> is a special tree that lifts the seeing from a human <u>whisperer</u> to whom djinns present themselves. Aligned with phases of the moon, <u>djinns</u> will sometimes lift their glamour and reveal themselves to a whisperer, who may be a person or an animal. <u>Whispering</u> is a hereditary trait. A whisperer fatigued with the seeing may dispel of it through a separation tree that makes itself known to the whisperer.

Then she started noticing the trees. Like the stumpy stout one along her tram ride to work—its leaves looked like a bad haircut. And the reaching tree—no matter how far she got, it kept nearing. She finally brought herself to touch its bark, expecting... what? A spark? A zing? Nothing happened. She scratched off a piece of its bark, put it on her tongue. It tasted of wintergreen, worse when she chewed it and it released a bitter sawdust. Her stomach hurt and she had the runs. That's all that happened, nothing eldritch.

So she was wary with the gnarly whorly thing halfway down the botanical gardens toward the nymphaea lily lake. That one came and went many times in her dreams. On an alpine trail one weekend, miles out from civilization, she powerwalked to avoid getting a stroke. There, she saw the monster oak swollen into a pregnant mud hut with a black hole for a door. Oh, she also saw the cobra tree. Dotted with tiny black eyes and a dangle of forked-tongues, branches that slithered towards her in the wind and she squealed. She did stop by the hugger tree along the gorge walk, but its scaly bark scratched her cheek. She ignored the cadaver tree, arms akimbo, tits out, a brush between its legs, but she did look at the hair-down witch tree that first startled before it pulled your gaze and you felt sage, stupid or both.

Neither one of those trees was a separation tree. She'd know if it were, wouldn't she? She didn't know. She tried telling Pepo about the trees but all he noticed were the dogs. The flappy-eared Labrador that cocked its head, then fun-loped to chase a twirling leaf. The red terrier all stocky and muscle—it growled when Pepo passed the girl owner, all nose and thumbs in her smartphone. The German shepherd puppy was not at all militant, simply soft and curious, and Zeda wanted to pet it. It was okay to notice dogs. What worried was Pepo's hungry look at each doggo. Like he wanted to eat it. Even the black pug and its snotty muzzle face.

Despite Pepo's deforming, his starving looks at the dogs, she begged and wailed as he left. Clung to his calf but it slimed in her hands, snailed over his abandoned moccasin on her doormat to join his parting self at the gate.

Overnight he'd stripped Zeda's heart to an expiration date, carpeted her devotion with a second-hand rug burrowed with dust, whorled with mould. The fungi came in the colour of an aurora that followed the pattern of her grief. She sat in silence at the folding table in her kitchen after he left. The house felt empty. Whitewashed. She sat in that kitchen until the whitewash dimmed and his moccasin outside the door obscured.

She's on an island again, one in which something's broken. It could be a promise, not a collective. It's a country or a coat, a shop sealed up with planks. She swallows and wonders what's been handed down, mother to daughter since she dropped out of the womb. She feels at gunpoint, or needlepoint, her body bobbing in a wreck, and every bone and belief is broken. She needs a ship at night, passing in the distance, careful not to hulk her plank where she'll leap into the blue-bright waters full of magpies and rudiments so close to the coast.

She tried reading online stories, but there was no map or carriage of words out of her mess. She was at a point it was too late to find a new protagonist. She had to work with what the 'plot unfold' offered. Even the signal on her laptop grappled with recall and she couldn't log online to swipe another body right. For they were all just bodies. And she was no wise-cracking detective to know any better, to carefully plan and develop fulsome sketches. So when the knock came and it was a postie, she took a beer from the fridge and asked if he'd drink it before she signed for her parcel.

She's not sure those were her words, but they were awkward either way. He took a swig and blew bubbles, scribbled something in a spiral-bound notebook.

Later, she ventured outdoors to delete the silence of his questioning eyes. She wore a raincoat on a wet-free day. She walked around the block and visited the café with soft lights, ebony and russet décor, and all polished wood. The café also had a goldfish. There was a haloumi on special, but she ordered a bag of crisps in a flavour that shouldn't exist. And a mocha. She leaned to tap her bank card and, when she looked up, the cashier's eye rolled. Off the socket, down his face.

His lopsided grin was not unfriendly, nor was his tail, as it rubbed itself at her feet. It left a trail of slime as it followed her home.

Now she sits down with time and wonders when she first noticed the others. After the cashier at the café, there was the ash-haired man with black-rimmed spectacles on TV. He was talking about industrial waste, biofuel and synthetic beef when his mouth fell. There was the sweet old lady on the train—one minute she was knitting her ride, next she was all eyes and teeth, ripping into a cat that was mostly fur and tail. Until all that remained was a skeleton, clean as a fishbone.

No-one else heard the whispers. They didn't see what she saw. They frowned at her meltdowns when pieces of people she met broke off or oozed, straight after whispers. It wasn't always murmuring. Sometimes it was black light. It had no name, just endless footsteps within footsteps to a place she'd never know, to a man she'd never see. She heard them everywhere: behind the abstract painting of a splash on the wall at the museum. Between hotel blinds—she shook them, nothing there. Outside her neighbour's window, underneath the pane. Inside the iron as she straightened the collar or sleeve of a blouse.

All she saw was a flicker of dusky light at the edge of her eye, then a turn of keys and moccasined feet walking, walking away.

Away.

It was a cold day in early March, she was out jogging. The reckoning in her head, an interminable wave of whispers and feet, was louder than she remembered. Her brain was a hive and a great big giant in wedged moccasins or heels was stamping at it. *Bzzzz! Splat!* Whisper, whisper—sentences that declared nothing. It didn't diminish the bees. They got more agitated, and the giant more keen. *Bzzzz! Splat!* Whisper, whisper. *Heya ho*, said a man walking his dog. In utter despair, she leaned against a tree near the botanical gardens, and plunged into it. It was an ordinary gum tree, nothing like the giant fungus she'd seen at the Dandenongs. This mundane eucalypt just opened its blackness and swallowed her. She fell into a spin, churning at speed. She felt stretched and pulled, rinsed and drained, like when her house wore her. It went on and on, speedy, slow—who cared? Something was killing her—that, she bloody cared.

She doesn't remember much about joy. But she does remember a distant memory of contentedness at the bloom of a wildflower, at the chirrup of a plump-crested robin, the butter-pecan drip of sticky ice cream down her fingers under the yellow sizzle of a summer sky. Looking back, she thinks of her heart racing, her whole body shaking at the sight of a full moon. When that happened, she lost diplomacy and words tumbled out of nowhere—she said zebra, gunboat or shit. She imagines herself as a ballerina anchored inside a colossal lamp serenading her with arias. Keeping her company, busy together before the rain.

Stretched and pulled, rinsed and whole. *Heya ho.* Whisper, whisper. Messages that made sense by the time the tree spat her onto a bridge. A restless bridge is the kind, here, there, you'd rather not boot across it. Not today, not any day. Or night. She paused as it creaked, recognising the smell, yet not seeing him. Pepo? Or was it Baba?

She stood barefoot under the moon, on the bridge from her misplaced life. She suddenly understood that she was a whisperer. One of those whisperers who saw things, heard things, no-one else did. If she turned back... But the house where she lived (she refused to think of it as her house) was too quiet. It just wanted to wear her, and all that. This was a better place: in the outline of herself, away from all that was uncanny. Yet she felt splashed... and could still hear the whispers. Echoes, echoes... whorls and whorls eddying into a roar.

Zeda saw the light out of the tree. And like her own mother before her, she stepped into a new life.

Taking

Shape.

A life of the everyday. Wasn't that the café with the goldfish? She looked around. A red van swept past—the postie waved. She walked home, unmindful to smells or whispers.

And yet,

   And

      Yet.

Memories of the Old Sun

SOMETIMES you wish you were a biorobot. Unemotive, just 1s and 0s.

Your mother's words burn inside your mind: "People are laughing, others pitying. Mazu. Who'll wait on me?"

"I'm here, Mae."

"The journey is far over the seas from Konakri. Come visit before I die."

"I'll visit. I promise. And you're not dying."

"Stop giving me regret. When will you find a woman?"

"If you keep asking, I'll stop calling."

"*Aiii*, his truth comes out. He'll stop ringing."

"Are you telling the phone?"

"Who birthed you? I broke my back to raise you. Now you will kill me with regret."

"It's not like that, Mae."

"The girls here are budding. I'll negotiate a wife with a good stomach. It shows in the clan—the ones who can make babies."

"Stop it. Please."

"I know to pick the right girl. Breasts like papayas. Buttocks bigger than a pot."

"There's more to life than marriage."

An email from Jordan. In it, the photo of a marigold-eyed kitten, head cocked at the camera. You want to tell Mae about Jordan, but on a spell like today she's no listener.

You snatch yourself back to her lamenting. "Don't put me in mourning. Child, you're cutting me."

"Now you exagger—"

"There's the question of dowry."

"Is this what it's about, Mae? I'll send money."

"Of course I need money. The cows are sick. And the village's still growing—we need a well to water our yams. I told the pastor at the school—"

"The one I raised money for?"

"That one. I told the pastor I'd ask about the well."

"Being here doesn't mean I'm rolling in money."

"Now you think you're a big shot. That you can stop helping."

You sigh. Sending money home is a bottomless cup. The village, through your mother, makes it an inescapable yoke. She finally agrees to hang up, because you invent that it's midnight.

"It's night there," she says in wonderment. "Like here?"

"Yes, Mae." Your pretend yawn is loud. "And if I don't sleep, who'll make money for us tomorrow? Sooo tired."

"You take my advice—I don't want to suckle the whole village. Give me a grandchild."

"I hear you, Mae."

"By the gods, you'd better. *Mffyuu.*" She sucks her teeth, letting you know she's not letting it go.

Jazz knows sie's a variable. Sie has an inbuilt scrapbook filled with memories, sometimes rushing, often rusting. They twirl inside hir head. File cards full of deserts and hungriness clipped away from hir heart. They are from names in a grammar sie doesn't remember, childhood friends or secrets: Bug, Dyn, Cyclone, Bash, Allon, Prim, Krema...

Making a biorobot is genesis—not a six-day creation, rest on the seventh, but rather a Darwinian evolution, natural selection and all. You put each zygote under lights, spin it slowly to nurture its earliest developmental stage—the unique genome sequence of human and artificial intelligence. The right genetic signature is necessary to form memories derived from mainframes and natural evolution.

Malware botches some of the zygotes and they begin to show excessive individual thought, traces of zeitgeist. You vaporize most anomalies, rain them back into the network as gametes. It doesn't matter if they had a name—all zygotes have a name—you deal with anomalies and rename them. Hundreds of zygotes each in a simulated placenta inside pods. Newborn. But only the fittest shall live.

A biorobotics engineer wants no variants, for obvious reasons. Variants generate runaway events. They display ego amplitudes, heroism complexes and random hierarchies that are circular, never linear. Inevitably, and *it is* inevitable, they fall into abeyance, putting the system into chaos.

The system demands everything exists in one voice: muted and responding only to command. Clumsy ones hit the bin, disconnected before they break synchrony. Daily, the eyes of cameras shift in a sense of rhythm and whirr, a silent opera taking down each face that might embrace self-actualization outside the greater good.

Rebooting, tagging and personal monitoring fixes the flaws of milder anomalies. Interface deconstruction tears down alpha anomalies. Intervention nullifies discord, keeping the systems in a unity of purpose. It ensures no counterpoint, convolution or polyphony: just algorithms and intelligence.

You assign each newborn to a research station that you closely monitor across the first year of extrauterine development. Then they graduate to space research stations.

Sie remembers days of life and death when fate snatched sie away and sealed hir sorrow to an exact point. Days that were mistrials drowned in desire, studded with intersections where babies cried in syntax, never in melody, and lights pulsed but never turned red.

That phone chat with your mother... you hold your head in your hands. You feel like a sea putting on tides in the dark, draping whole cities, washing away last night's news and your mother's insistence.

"My blood and sweat under the old sun put you to school—see where you are now."

"And I'm grateful, Mae."

"When your father died, you became the head of the house. Don't you forget, son."

"I won't."

A new item on the taskbar. You click the email open. Another Jordan animated gif: 'Happy Lunch Hour!' It's shaped in old gold on a beach speckled with palm trees. He fills you with good vibes.

Memory is snow—iced crystals falling in clusters from the sky. Pellets big as fists, opaque yet trustless. Emotions are surface, doorsteps of a moment.

There was a time when conversation with your mother was easy. But on the phone it's crumbs and shapes, what's left of language and duty. If your mother were on social media, you'd take your chances on texting. IDK, BRB, G2G. You'd get away with saying TTYL, promising to talk later, and not doing it. Maybe she'd get the idea with YGTI.

You chuckle softly, but it's only with imagining her texting you back: *WTF? YOLO. Give grandchild. ASAP.* Indeed, one only lives once. You've never been much of a swimmer yet dive into the ocean on your small screen, away from a weight of responsibility. Tradition is a beast. Why must you marry? Marriage is antiquity. There's no alchemy for a perfect one. What you remember of your parents is absence. Your father was always away. Mostly for work, sometimes with other women. You remember the fighting like thunder—you trembling under a bed as Mae and your father crashed, wrestling around the house, breaking things. You don't want to be that.

You're unhappy, but Jordan's meme that's an animated gif of huggy cartoony figures in metallic hues and pearly textures, jellybean shaped, is lifting.

At nights sie wakes up from pixelated cyclones in hir dreams, shapeless footsteps to hir world of amorphous vapours. Hir life is a cradle— forming, morphing hir newborn self until sie toddles out of it. Hir heart is a blizzard—the data it holds veers from science, erodes trust. It's a heart that touches petals with fists, unclear where on a flower to caress. If sie could levitate, sie'd give hirself to all the books in the universe,

26

speak their tongues. Sie'd teach hirself magic from a book, pull out
ebony rabbits and gilded coins that look easy on satellite.

Your eyes turn back to the job. 24/7 on live feed and reruns, no
popcorn. A silver and black grid of the universe. A switch on the control
splashes colour if you wished it. You watch the biorobots in their tasks
across the globe. Inbuilt to take temperature, pressure, rain and wind
readings. They're humanlike, no different from people on the streets. A
little sentient, yet designed to be windvanes, barometers, wet and dry
bulbs through human skin. They're imprinted with aerial surveillance
and radius maps, motion imagery and billions of pixels in resolution
splashed on your screen.

You created them. Still, sometimes you pity them. Isolated in
research stations across the globe. You have four primes: Jazz, Krema,
Cyclone and Bash. First-year wards in the biorobotic flock. Jazz is in
Antarctica—sie was always different but you gave hir a chance from
deconstruction. You remember how sie was always clingy, wanting a
song, a cuddle or whatnot reassurance to perform hir best. The others
don't worry you: Krema in Pelican Point, Namibia—sand-dune-filled,
blazing hot oasis, miles of desert. Cyclone in Mawsynram, East India—as
wet as it comes on the East Khasi Hills district. Bash in Death Valley,
Eastern California—it's a furnace creek there. The government calls
it Nextgen 4.0, but is it a future that you want? Each biorobot is a
humanesque quantum machine.

Still, you worry about Jazz.

Jordan sends you a video funny of a big-bottomed man in blood-red
dungarees dancing 'Jingle Bells' to an afro beat called ndombolo.

Sie remembers a world awash with sound. It feels years away, but
sie remembers it. Sometimes whoosh... whoosh, or thump... thump...
Always lub dub lub dub. Now and then a voice, hushed. Every now
and then a whirr or a buzz, a hum or a drone. Sometimes beep, beep.
Sie remembers jumping at a touch from outside the membrane. A
gentle rub, and a song. Sie neared. Pressed hir ear to feel, to listen to
the world. Hir world now. Entering it was calm in a squeeze, and then

cold, then rub, more rub. And then warm full of soft. Rhythm. Melody.
A fuzzy that never lasts. Hir poetry of yearning.

Another Jordan funny on your phone screen is dappled with heart shapes and ruby roses.

You crave sunshine. You long for the sun back home in Konakri. You step away from the monitors, go out the door. But outside is no sun. It's full-blown winter, people in coats walking away from you on the streets. Cyclists in spandex jingle bells at drivers and shenanigans of life in the slow lane.

You smoke the city, packs of it a day. Not real darts. You stand outside the burnt-brick monolith of your workplace, same time each mid-morn, puffing the world. A few times to get going, until you feel cafés, libraries, theatres, high rises, post-offices, even ICUs—too many of them—on your tongue. You let the traffic jams and politicians linger in your mouth, telecom poles, museums, thugs, buskers, beggars, nurses, teachers wafting in too. You cast your mind on the taste of the metropolis to its last despondence, discontent, fear, fury and all. But sometimes there's awe, serenity and hope. You draw the last bit into your mouth.

At first, when you started the smoke—Jordan introduced you to it, smoking the city, as he called it—you felt dizzy, nauseous. Jordan held you as you gagged. But over time the sensation of motion sickness morphed into something complex. What you feel now is alertness. You feel real. Relaxed, away from family pressure. You feel a pleasure of yearning, a nostalgia of curiosity. But you never want anyone other than Jordan to see you like this.

Yebe! Hey you! Found a woman yet? Your mother in your head disturbs the peace of the moment. You return inside to monitor the research stations.

Your phone vibrates. It's Jordan.

"Hiya," he says.

'Hello you. How's the writing going?"

"Going," he says. "You know how it is. What's happening there?"

You want to talk about your mother, but don't. Instead, you tell him about your dream. "I was a goddess looking for new suns. Not one sun, a whiteness that's all colours of the rainbow. I was searching for many suns. Different colours."

"Right."

"I was sick of same old. What I needed was blue. A teal sun, or a chocolate cherry one. I got close to my quest but shifted into a bird. It was a bird that kept morphing. First, I was a hyacinth macaw, cobalt blue feathered. Then I was a quetzal—scarlet, indigo and olive green with a white underside on my tail.'

"I'd love to see your underside tail," says Jordan.

"And then I was a red-crested turaco. Green bodied, white-faced. Running on the ground, not flying in the skies, but in sonic speed. I was screeching and jabbering, whooping out my search for the suns. It's a prophecy, do you think?"

"More like, they say dreams tell us something about ourselves."

You look at the monitors.

Sie remembers Daddy.

You made the biorobots feel safe in an engineered womb, birthed them and threw them into experiments. You trained and tested each biorobot for endurance. You shoved them into water and studied their comfort, breathing, how they positioned for buoyancy. You stuffed them in saunas and monitored their need for water, which ones—like Jazz—lost their cool. You threw them into labs swollen with sandstorms, and observed their natural compass, which ones stayed hungry yet measured. You cut off their oxygen, nearly crushed them with pressure. You studied their navigation, patience, inventiveness.

But you don't want them speculating why penguins make a beeline down a sandy hill. That's the ilk of sentience you tried rebooting out of Jazz. Sie reminds you of a bee.

Memory is a billion miles folded in a box. It's tucked inside a key at zero degrees staring long and hard at a wish for a bee. Because a bee prefers a garden or an orchard, a meadow or a copse—everywhere sie wants to be. Because a bee likes dandelions and black-eyed susans, and the bittersweet

*breath of a bouquet is better than decay. Because a bee is dusky and blond,
burgundy and silver, auburn and lime, azure, even lilac: none of those
hues in this dull world and its swirl of winds. Because a bee makes honey,
and it is thick and golden and tastes like a quest. Because a bee makes a
buzz, and that's a ringing in hir head sie can explain.*

Yes. Jazz reminds you of a bee. Because a bee stings, and a sting is
true evidence that you feel. How do you apologise to a biorobot you
have created? In the world of research and engineering, apology is a
hypocrite or a shadow or a make-shift desk with no authority. Apology
is no answer for that which wants to come in and close the door behind
it, leaving you trapped. Apology has no neat machine language, just a
lisp. It might inhabit a name but casts adrift as a rowboat you swim and
swim towards but can never reach it in your dream. Apology is a face
in a hurricane, and it looks like your mother, drowning you. You look
wrong and ridiculous questioning it, even drunk or alien, across a world
of stories there and then, here and now.

You can't apologise, same way you can't tell your mae the truth. You
live in two worlds, and you feel a deep and terrible sadness about that.
When you leave each world, you carry boxes cramped with deception,
trickery and guile encamped with sprites who make hostages from what
matters. You're a god or a goddess who sows souls from shore to shore,
fiddling away from chaos and grief. Swooping music vibrates in circles,
rips and ripples, as the rest plod with sprites and souls, and the fiddle
pecks, prods and cripples.

On a scale of 1–10, it feels like 0.

Before Jordan, you secured the walls of your heart so nothing new
blew in, nothing old blew out. All that was left was reclaimed baggage
occupying objects of memory never in use, simply recycled along
undesignated revelations. What you needed was a blanket: washable,
breathable, lightweight in summer, plush in winter. That blanket was
Jordan. He saw through the flicker of light on the hourglass of your
armour that suggested the straps were not made of steel but rather fairy
floss. You were fragile, sickly sweet and poor for your health. You had
only to let in Jordan, and everything changed.

You wonder why you didn't tell Jordan about the other dream. The one where your goddess walked with a gap across a city choked in smoke, and theories flew about the cavernous hole in her torso. Tar-shined ravens and death-watch beetles also soared through it. No one offered a mist blanket so she could fold her wings at midnight. She looked at herself and muttered a prayer or a dream. She gave anyone who looked an opus of her hollow.

Sie wears an infinite new coat over hir old coat. It's unrecorded, no assumptions. When summer... if summer... long days, dropping nights. When spring... if spring... Hir heart is sealed in envelopes to a city of new suns.

There's a deadness about the night, yet you pick at it. You feel a dirge inside, yet you're not good at chanting. You distract yourself with motion imagery from Krema, Cyclone, Bash and Jazz in their routines around their meteorological stations. Krema—unmindful of pink flamingos, black jackals and fur seals only miles north in Walvis Bay—mono-focused on iron-coloured sand dunes in Namibia. Cyclone—neutral to calcareous caves and rocky waterfalls, ferns, even orchids and aroids of the sacred forest in nature's museum—collecting water and measuring rain in East India. Bash—impartial to salt flats, sand dunes, canyons, lakes and craters—simply charting dryness and windspeed in California.

I milked goats, says your mae in your head. *Took the produce, together with mangoes and tomatoes, to the stall in the market for your schooling.*

And I thank you, Mae.

Krema, Cyclone and Bash go about unquestioning of their lesser tasks, compliant that you will situate them to their higher purpose. But Jazz is different. As sie goes about hir climatological tasks in Antarctica, sometimes you notice a sadness in sie, and a happiness—the break of a smile, a spring in hir step—when sie integrates with nature. Sie sleeps under stars, swims in iced waters, gawks at penguins, feels snow on hir tongue.

You watch the screens. None of the biorobots can hear you and the hypersonic imprints of your invisible chant.

The place that reminds sie of home has deserts and seas. They scorch or hump in scars and pleas. Sie drags hir heart through heavens and earths in endless quests to find holy burghs. But what sie sees are memories and visas to the universe.

Jordan emails you a sample of his writing. "It's called 'Damned, More Than Thirty Percent'," he says. It reads:

Your body's flamboyant with tonight's headlines. An unruly bugaboo peers through the sight: X marks the spot.

You bob through the city, in, out of back streets, away on the freeway. But it's coming for you: the ghost of your harming... all glaring in half-light.

"It's called prose poetry," he says. "The rogue cousin of a poem and flash fiction. I wrote it for you—there's more in the head, Mazu. Think I'll make it big?"

"You'll be right."

"The text's spooky."

What spooks you more are your mae's words in your head: "Your children will do for you what you're failing me."

You fold away each memory of the old sun that's black frost, but can't escape it. Like the goddess in your dreams, you want new suns. You'd happily start again with no expectation of what's normal, each moment that happens.

CCTV, no popcorn. You look at the screen. This here is getting by. Is this how you want to live your life—getting by?

A bird on Jazz's screen catches your eye. It's running extremely fast on the ground, until it stops in front of Jazz. How the? In Antarctica? More so, you're fascinated by hir response to it. You watch with curiosity as sie reaches hir hand to the red-crested turaco.

It's green bodied, white-faced. It perches on hir shoulder. Sie hums. It screeches, jibbers, like a jungle monkey. They practice a shared language, something intuited from intrinsic selves. It's a wordless language cast from simple lives, complex to forget. But words never stay dormant long. They sear patterns in the snow, disrupt the icy water's rhythm. Jazz and the bird follow each other distances along the shore, hear voices in the wind, and they remember. It doesn't matter who speaks first. The turaco tells sie about luck and choice.

Sie hums.

It's grey and wet driving home. It feels like solstice, the longest and shortest day, all at once. The wipers go *lub dub lub dub* like a heartbeat. Or the sound of drowning.

What you get when you turn the handle and cross the threshold into your shared flat is a warm, sweet aroma of your mae's kitchen.

"I looked it up on the net. Got pumpkin leaves, cassava and curry from an African market in Clay. Drove miles to reach it. Sorry, no tilapia. I got a porcelain pot to bake it with chicken. Smells right, you think?"

"Always."

Jordan's smoky eyes put embers into your body, shimmers in all your senses. You hug him, notice base notes of wood, cypress and earth in his aftershave.

"How can you be taller than this morning when I left? What you been up to?"

He laughs. "You're not the only specialist around here. Writers do spells all the time. Know that?" His shoulders are broader, a few inches more. He carries them right, no big boy guns on his muscles—he goes easy in the gym. There's spunk in his boyish face, tenderness too when he looks at you, as he is now. "Think dinner can wait?"

Stroking fingers scorch away each longing for solitude and in its place blossom orchids into your heart. Luminescent stars, triple moons. You abandon independence and capitulate to the explosions of a galaxy inside your flesh.

Later, much later, you sit together on the high-rise balcony, smoking the city and its silver rain and blinking lights. Tonight, the metropolis has forgotten the taste of politicians and guile, traffic jams and disconnect. What it offers is the promise of morning dew. A new beginning.

You think about the biorobots. Already you know that Krema, Cyclone and Bash will graduate with soaring colours to the space research stations. Jazz—you don't know about sie. Jazz has excessive individual thought and, as a biorobotics engineer, you know there's one way to deal with that.

But sie's more than 1s and 0s. Sie's a spirit of age. Funny, it doesn't worry you now. It doesn't matter anymore about counterpoint, convolution or polyphony. So what? There's diversity in algorithms and intelligence, and what's wrong with difference? Would it be so foolish of you, perhaps, if you asked Jazz what sie wants to do with hir life? See what random sie comes up with.

Sie opens hir memories. Colour photographs tacked close to hir heart. Nothing in particular, just dirt roads to a day that's coming. It's full of songs and dragons. Sie's the one who sees ghosts, who walks on water in hir sleep. The child from a cerulean pearl yet smouldering with phoenix wings. Sie loves Daddy and his folding arms, the careful way his eyes chorus. Will the leaves bud, and the flowers open one by one? Sie walks in hir sleep, or is sie a ghost of hirself? There's no password to reset.

Thank you for sharing, jibbers the turaco. And never a ghost.

You miss the splendour of an African vista darker than tar. The starry nights and bush calls of the savanna. The moon's gaze on the regal height of baobab trees. You wonder how that would taste.

"Perhaps soon enough when you visit," says Jordan. You look at him, startled. "Speaking out loud, mate."

"Let's play *Imagine*," you say.

"You start."

"Imagine we're sitting in an air-loft garden atop a magellanic cloud orbiting the Milky Way," you say.

"Imagine the petal of a whirlpool flower wafting inward from an ultraviolet vista and reaching your soul," says Jordan.

"Imagine you're for life."

Jordan's smile is full of glitter. He feels like sunlight. You wonder if something this perfect could go wrong. He's the summer that gives you reason to wake each dawn. You tell him about Mae wanting you to marry, have children.

"I don't make much money," he says, dancing rays in his eyes. "I can't bear you any babies, but I can cook—that do?"

You join in his laughter, at first uneasy, then you settle into belly-deep mirth that pushes out tears in its high.

"Will you tell her?" Jordan asks, a glisten in his eyes too.

You look at him. "Righto. Tomorrow, I will." You clasp his hand. "Ace."

"Would you—" you stammer at his raised brow, "like, maybe... I was thinking video call... like, um." The words rush out: "Shall we tell her together?"

"Sure thing. That's decent." He squeezes your hand.

"Serious?"

"I'm all in. A video is worth a thousand words, right?" The sun in his eyes.

"Dude, just don't kiss me."

Your laughter is together.

Now it's Jordan's turn to study you. "She'll pull through."

"You reckon? I've given so much. Surely, she can allow me this little happiness."

"Little?" He roughs you up, you roll on the floor giggling.

She'd be wounded, maybe mad. She might not speak to you for days, weeks, maybe months. But you'd send money, then you'd call. She'd tell you about how you were hard to come out, nearly killed her birthing you. How she didn't ask for the curse that closed her womb after one tiny child—look how you've grown. She'd get cunning, like a fox, go spiritual or ideological, tell you about so and so's daughter in the village. You'd distract her with the trickery of a hare, and gently remind her about Jordan.

The phone rings, and you let it. You stand at the balcony watching the road, as a silver sky in the vista reaches with its doubling rain. You hope that you'll dream many suns in all directions and a kaleidoscope panning out softly. That you'll sleep in late and wake in a tousle of toes and a smiling noon reeling towards Eden.

When the Wind Blows

NO ONE SAID this was a ghost train but it feels like it.

The truth in the mirror is full of lies that don't like the crow lines around her eyes. There's a sound in her ear on a code-breaking frequency. Keys pop in random, decoding something she doesn't know. A conversation's happening in her head, to which she's not privy. It goes to a ring, a whistle of air. And, like the crypto keys, endless.

Suyema walks along the Great Eastern as oversized trucks with beamer lights judder by. Everything drives dangerously. Nothing gives way. She sees too late the signpost: *Loose gravel on the footpath*. But she walks on, past the *Wrong way / Go back* sign and the *Hand car wash* sign. Turns when she reaches the mini shopping centre with its *TAB* and *Thirsty Camel*, and a grocery selling mangoes with a sweet smell of home.

Back in her cottage an angry shower spits on the roof two minutes straight. Then all is silent but for a jumping beetle exhausting itself on her timber floor. She takes a pan and hand broom, scoops it out the door into tepid air.

The mozzies are half-hearted—the odourless guard from the local store smells discounted. Should have used the lavender repellent. Something annoying bites her scalp, palms and heels in a persistent way that she's not. She infuses her body with family protection, low irritant. Oblivion presses inside her eyeballs, blood in her sinus.

She reads and re-reads weeks of J's wooing texts from when they met at the chocolate factory, swapped numbers. "You're my queen," he says in one.

She looks at the photo that fell out of his Facebook page.

She'd taken an Uber down Roe Highway into West Swan Road and its shoulders of trees fully green in a scorcher summer, rode all the way into Perth's Valley of Taste. Suyema got off at the chocolate factory, and that's where they first met—staring at the Chokka Quokka. They both laughed. J took her hand, put cocoa nibs into them.

"Crushed cocoa beans."

"For what?"

"Smoothies, whatever."

"Why should I care?"

"Antioxidants—fab for the heart. Cures cancer."

"Do I look like I'm sick?"

"Far from it."

She followed him to the red grape chocolate shelf and they lingered at the freckled hampers.

"Look, luscious liquorice," said J. "Just like you."

"What—250g boxed or bagged?"

He smiled, put a ruby taster on her tongue—it was sweet and sour with berry undertones.

He bought her a chocolate liqueur. "Just like you," again, he said.

"You see me as a night-cap. Straight from the bottle, over ice-cream with cold milk?"

"Rich. Dark. Silky."

It didn't matter she knew nothing about J. He was homecoming. She'd been prodigal all her life, now she had arrived. Who thought she'd find love on this writer's retreat that was initially giving nothing, until she went gallivanting?

It wasn't merely that they met at a chocolate factory but that they visited together the stall that sold the seeing. It was halfway between *Kwik Koffee* and *Honey Fresh*. They fell laughing into a pop-up stall named *A Lick of Lavender*. It housed an aproned man in jean shorts, lavender thongs and a lavender T-shirt. His eyes—she tried to remember his eyes but couldn't. His was a gaze that asked a question, told an answer, said never mind and she felt at home. It re-routed her thinking to the same place twice. Jean shorts. Thongs. Lavender T-shirt. Those eyes—she tried to remember his eyes, but they touched her needy gut and said never mind to the likelihood of rain.

He reminded her of a medicine man back home who touched her when she was little. She'd walked barefoot with her mother under a scorching sun, panting up a hill of red clay. It was speckled with twisted rocks and fallen leaves from forked trees, all naked. They reached his hut, not much of it. He stood in his loin cloth, shook a calabash over her head, chanted, and spit flew. He laid hands on her head, then gave her mother smoked herbs to stop Suyema's bed-wetting. The taste was tangy, peppery; the smell grated her very core, and she fought life and death each time her mother neared with the foul crush. But whatever it was— the chants or the herbs—it worked.

That's what it was: the Lavender man reminded her of touch, of a herb that worked. It rekindled a longing for home. She remembered the whispering that climbed from her mother's grave perched with ravens. Is that why she fled across seas? To forget the missing?

A Lick of Lavender sold boutique lavender: massage lavender in baby vases; hand-made lavender candles; hand and body lotions in petite lavender jars on top of a wine barrel. She bought a refresher spray and a natural insect repellent labelled *family protection*. It even had pulse point oil in a fairy bottle.

"For headaches and stress," the man said in an accent she couldn't place.

"Look, it has soya bean and olive oil," said J.

"Table for two?" the strange man said. The stall was tiny, but suddenly they were sat in a cushy lavender sofa with a purple velvet curtain behind. And there was more than one table, real palm trees growing between them.

The man served them lavender tea. It was floral, a hint of rosemary, green apple and soil. Suyema noticed, as if for the first time, he was short-cropped, face covered in hair speckled with salt.

She didn't think twice about the fairy bottle the man pressed into her palm, as J paid the bill. "One lick and the wind blows," the man said.

She wondered if he understood that she might be stressed about the writing, but was astonished to discover it wasn't pulse point oil but rather labelled: lavender truth serum.

Suyema didn't know whose truth, or how.

Now she knows. One lick, nothing happened, until she logged on social media. She'd gone online many times, zilch—until the lick.

She curls into a doona, hugs the pillow. The photo she saw... A child is innocent, a child is a gift. It's a child she's just met.

Suyema feels a deep and terrible sadness. She contemplates the chubby-lipped bub in princess pink, laying on its back and sucking a thumb. So full of trust in a sleepy-eyed gaze at the hidden one behind the camera.

How does a man *not lead with that*?

Back home people understood your truth from a handshake. You went out with one whose family you knew. A person knocked on your door, and the whole village entered with its nose. A gift of cows secured trust. Duty. You gained an onus to make your house stable, to love your family with your heart, blood and core. This was how you paid homage to the ancestors. It was how a person's name lived.

She and J skipped the handshake. They'd leapt from laughter to a bed. In a motel. Lots of messaging in between. That's what people did here: texting. You didn't have to know their family.

Dawn.

Colour dissolves into pallid blue, then silver, then sunflower. From the writer's desk a slanted oak, fork trunked. The doleful wail of a black cockatoo. Hers is a space enamoured with a hound's tooth—not the personal starship of a bounty hunter, or the duotone textile pattern in black and white. More the clean as a hound's tooth allegory for a protagonist in a crime scene, yet free of wrongdoing.

But there's dissonance in this story that works better as a prose poem.

Backspace.

She takes it all out on a mango. Draws its skin and bites into flesh. Suddenly she feels more homesick. She presses with her fingers, devours the fragrant ooze of its innards. She pushes her teeth all the way to its husk, lets the wet drip onto a manuscript that pays no heed to what she feels.

She doesn't remember what distracts her—the sound of a humming fan or her empty heart. Right now she's lost sight of entrancement. And the way she gouges out the seed of a harmless fruit points to an unnamed catastrophe, or temporal madness based on a memory she can't grasp.

J is no homecoming. She feels a deep disconnect.

Family is everything.

How does a man not lead with *that*?

The Shimmer

THE DRIZZLE gets heavier. The grass, a slippery locust full of green. The game's on Big-O's boot. He's a picture of concentration. Friday night footy, the crowd's red hot. Fans loving a kicker. And they know Big-O's not a rookie. He's a top player in career form. A god on the field.

He positions. Looks at the posts, sprays a beaut around the corner.

He nails it! cries the commentator. *Right on top of his game!*

Fire through the foot! agrees another. *No problems at all!*

Big-O's lap around the field. The crowd's worship under the stadium's floodlights.

Fontasia's a stoner. Her normal life's head-fogged. She pulls a dart—it's dope, as in awesome. The first high hits her into a nest of demons. Red glows in their stares, frozen in partial eclipse. Around their shadows she's blushing meat infused with wattleseed. When she sees the shimmering man in a scatter of light, she knows he's random. She sorta hates it. Feels like a rip-off, this saving by a random from a red glow of demons aiming to devour her.

But it's subtly different, to an extent. Lacks imagination—how the vision vacillates between light and fog. She sees her reflection on the demon's charcoal tongues, their fangs, before the shimmer boils over, ashes them amidst howls.

Big-O dances easy in the rain with the ball. He likes to make early

41

statements like this, waltzing to goals, basking in the crowd's adulation as cameras and light towers wink.

Norton sends a pass. *Neat and tidy!* says the commentator.

It's pure!

Big-O kicks the distance, splits the middle of the posts.

Too fierce!

What a freak!

Seems seconds, he's at it again. Boak—rastas and all—slides the ball across on a ground-level legger. Big-O runs to meet it in top gear. Snatches momentum, discipline off the tip of his foot. Caresses the ball through the post.

Quick smart! cries the commentator into the mike.

That. Was. Terrific!

She didn't go for Big-O 'cos he's banked. Sure, he rolls Fontasia's habit, only he doesn't know it. Outside the footy with him, she parties next level hard. No idea of timelines or weekdays, laundry or vacuuming. After each shindig with randos, mostly when Big O's on training, she floats in a gathering of pissed people at a park. It rocks good. Big-O doesn't mind not finding her home. And she knows the trick to his core—take-in from a joint named Pablos. It has waffles and thickshakes. Cheesed-up fries sandwiched in glazed donuts.

"Wouldn't it be nice if they served this with a line of icing?" she once said to Big-O.

"Could have ordered, why didn't you?" he said, unclued to the line or icing she meant.

She likes how he says, "If you ask what type of food I am, I'm bread. Never known anyone to piss off a loaf. I've got sixth sense: I see bread people."

But she's totally not bread people. Nor are his friends. They're a fucking mercenary gang—Boak, Norton, King Charlie. They're fisters, absolute knuckles. Bullshitters too. They talk shit and you think they're fucking inspiration. But they're bull, alright, like seriously. Yet ... watch them goal side.

Such a beautiful leg! What a good-looker! the commentator cries.

It's insane! An absolute ripper!

They know how to spread points on the board, snappers to the last minute. Goals flying from heads and knees. Who makes something out of nothing? They do. But everyone knows it's on Big-O. He makes it happen. Runs on nuclear. Slams it on the boot through the post, on the back of fantastic.

King Charlie whacks a bender over his head. Norton's on a bolter that gives Big-O the act. Big-O leans back.

He starts right, the commentator says.

Always spot on!

Without looking, Big-O steers the ball above the umpire's hat.

Knows his way around the sticks, cries the commentator.

He's kicked that well enough!

Fontasia's unsure of herself. She blusters through life, buried in blossom and litter. She swaps faces, no options before committing. Slips off the old, slips in the new—it's necessity or chance. There's no room for discerning—it's how she survives. This is the year, the year, the year... she hums to herself, waiting for a break. Who's playing hide and seek? She counts to a hundred. Another hundred. Yet another, before she opens her eyes to a new passport. Big-O puts her right. Like that time at Lake Weeroona... they had pistachio ice cream, hazelnut, butterscotch. She stood with him. Together at dusk they watched black ducks, black cormorants, black swans. The hairy-headed grebe, a white-faced heron, too. They looked for the ibis and the pelican, but the birds had gone gallivanting for blue-green algae.

The waitress at a café called When We Hustle—surrounded by blond-leafed trees, and offering Zen yoga—asked: "Any special requirements?"

"What? No. That's ridiculous," said Big-O. But he was smiling.

"No," said Fontasia. She looked out past a lone bench by the lake, and autumn's brown scatter on the green, at a misty-leaf tree drooping from the shores into the waters. Nearby, a huddle of red-billed water birds.

"I've been caught before asking for special requirements," Big-O was saying. "They gave me an alternative even a dog won't eat."

"What I mean is... allergies," said the waitress.

"Nah. Don't talk shit like that, mate," said Big-O. He laughed, eyes on Fontasia. "I can say *she's* allergic," he nodded at Fontasia. "To my aftershave. But we won't be eating it."

Fontasia ordered a rare fillet. "Do you have wattleseed?"

The waitress stayed with a blank face. "No. Sorry."

Big-O gobbled sweet potato pizza with smoked gouda. "Smooth and twined in eggplant." He looked at Fontasia, picking at asparagus around her steak. "I thought you were vegan."

"I am."

Turned out to be one of those tired evenings. Back in the hotel, they watched a B-grade horror movie that relied on drum scares. Music scores that made you jump.

It was chill, like vibing. Big-O was the elements, brimming fire and ocean, blizzard and air. She looked at him askance, sighing and shaking, knowing better than to succumb, but she did. With him she floated the universe in spaceless time, screening memory from feeling and filaments of the lunar spirit. Unable to wrestle the hallucinations and a sunset of fear that Never

Left.

He toyed with her sea-green hair that reminded her and made her forget she was merfolk.

The rain has stopped, the grass still wet. Another ball sails through the middle.

Game ho!

He's a son of Zeus, or what?!

When Fontasia's mother died, she felt unhinged yet preserved in winter-bites. Neighbours came to pay last respects, but it was really to remind her of her jeopardy: her shattered connection to the merworld. Not long before they pushed her to the edge of the otherworld, she mused, as she stared at the bare living room, stark-naked without her mother. She wished patterns of familiarity on the mantelpiece, places her mother had touched, would pull out some tears. But she was too numb to cry. Her eyes were filled with jars of dried-up lexicons that needed nothing more than a market square.

The other team does some roaming, a fumble on the pitch. Someone puts the ball through. Now they're trading goals. Carnage on the injury front.

Big-O climbs out clean. Gives King Charlie a hand from the roughing-up pack.

The moon is blood weight, thinks Fontasia on another high. She sees folktales to the other side. No-one's supposed to laugh at frogs and weeds, kangaroo apples and river mists. She sees chooks, leopards and geckos inside the murals of a total lunar eclipse. Erhus whisper tales in visions of time. Orchestras and ensembles.

The referee holds up the ball for a toss. No-one's running, eyes intense on the ball. King Charlie gives the other team a stare. The referee throws the ball.

Players scatter in the wetness of play and defence.

Out in the middle, Big-O strolls out of nowhere. Serenades the ball, bursts with it into a sprint. Lines it up, hooks it home.

It's a cracker!

Bloody marvellous!

She's in a forest of underwater kelp. The sound of breakers smashing on a rock above. She opens her eyes to a barista handing her a mouse. It's blind and shrieking, animates her to understand. She knows the warning won't be the last but she's too distracted with humanitarian disasters to grasp instructions on the froth. She whisks out in her head a megachurch by the oceanfront. A preacher's sandstone castle with an infinity pool. Nonuplets begot in the pews, etymologically speaking. "I didn't do it," say all possible fathers, unremotely linked by blood, wealth or ideology to the rag-tag girl who doesn't know what to do, but in smoke and miracles contemplates revenge.

King Charlie kicks a flyer. Norton passes the ball to Boak, who does a special legger that gets the crowd going.

An absolute belter!
What a goal!
Big-O is there for Boak's leap-hug. King Charlie and Norton too ...
Unstoppable together.

Fontasia wonders why it's not the first time she's recollecting this vision or memory. Dusk taps gently at her door, but her world is gasping for shimmer. The soggy heat in the room from the heating isn't the first of warnings. The dishwasher hums in the background. It's on a timer—Big-O set it. A horseshoe of plates, knives and forks oblivious to matters surrounding questions as to how she is a fish that's lost its gills. Where has she put her skin?

Her skin is stone that needs no looking back. Her skin is a mother's dirge, a tidal wail that trails a hollow nest in the water's wake. Fontasia leans into a forgetting life, a future running deep into sweepstakes where there's only forwards, no backwards—even if it rains snakes.

She floats and drowns in displacements, debris full of lonesomeness in a language she doesn't understand. What she understands is a deep and terrible sadness. And she wonders if she'd do different if she lived again her epoch.

Right now, head-fogged, it's a nonverdict.

Big-O runs straight into a tackle, streams away. He's clean through the field. Puts the jets on, bends the ball through the goal.
Big-O puts on a masterclass! A banana on the run!
He's just a star! We love him!

When it comes to scales, denial takes a deep-held conviction, together with coping mechanisms that have a pretty good inkling where they're going: to a kitchen full of confidence beyond motivational slogans that are simply repression, and more refusal to face everlasting truth in an endless gruel.

The pale cottage died with her mother. First, it rattled, shuddered, then became rigor-mortised. It mildewed from pale brown to green-grey. Fontasia kept waiting for her mother to put a warm consoling hand on her shoulder... but nothing.

Mother

  was

    dead.

      Mother

...who tried to shield her from the maw of unbelonging.

Mother who'd finally perished of heart wear and dismay at the merworld's refusal to accept her flesh and blood. The conversations Fontasia had borne with herself her entire life became conversations with others. Their black eyes spoke and reminded her of the Empty, and it was a noun swollen with person, place and thing. The Empty was never abstract. It was fully compound, countable, collective. It was as concrete as birth. The Empty was as vivid as a lonely night, and it made her older, more crumpled, until she swam.

Soon as she came of age, she swam on the verge of tears from the cottage that was heart-worn, dismayed. Pulseless. She swam to find refuge from a life full of unwelcome, and was still swimming when, one night during a storm that wasn't a dream, she despaired. She gave herself up to hundred-year waves so they could break her, bone by bone.

After all she was a hybrid, an unlawful daughter of land and sea. One of nine weaklings, the only one that survived. Of her humanoid father she knew naught. She knew everything about her mother's disgrace, for sullying the bloodline. Any talk of love or lust was debris, evidence of collapse. Thinking of her tormented parentage she closed her eyes, allowed water nymphs to come and drag her to the kelp, and for a moment she churned.

No

  water

    nymphs

      came.

What Fontasia instead saw in her churn was a spear of light. Then she heard her name, saw its letters in white froth in the sea. Text reminded her to find home. Suddenly, warm and reaching light enveloped her, floated her to the sands of a rocky beach.

A flick out to King Charlie in control of the back half. Boak, Norton, King Charlie—all ace. Big-O gets the ball again.

It's bending, it's bending! cries the commentator. *All the time, bending!*

Two goals in a minute and a half!

The other team's coach, a man on the precipice, is shaking mad. Balls his fists, spews cuss words the tiny mike doesn't take.

Past impossible surf into the cove of a rugged coastline, she coughed up on a long beach. It gently sloped, splashed white in sand. She stepped out of the tide, astonished she was not a mermaid or a blobfish. She was human.

As human as the hunk of a man with a crew cut, wearing the body of a warrior and the eyes of a god of love and walking towards her. She promptly forgot the past and reached out for this man who held out a hand and contemplated her difference outside the water's conscious eye. He was a comfort. A reminder of Not Empty.

And though she was so far from home, she was not alone. They downed woodfired pizzas with cold craft beers at a waterfront pub. The gruyere on the thin crust was pregnant with sweet nut and earth, black olives and sundried tomatoes.

Big-O was ganged—with him Boak and his dreadlocks, ochre-tongued Norton and King Charlie, all big and ripple-muscled. They guzzled and gobbled, ordered more pizza and beer. They debated the flavour of goat cheese full of tart, silverbeet and broccolini under the waiter's bemused eye. Fontasia was conscious that, any moment, all might change.

But the man who was a comfort reminded her what else could happen. He took her to his ice-cold castle surrounded by poplars. Think of a castle without a moat, cannons or a great hall. Just sandstone and timber, wrought iron balustrades in a snake scale finish.

"You clean all this?" she asked.

"A cleaner comes in once a week."

She walked up a staircase winding along a wall intervalled with portraits of fading faces and headless busts: voluptuous, skinny, male, female, naked, clad. She climbed into a king bed with a velvet bedhead all classic grey, chrome studding on its upholstering.

It didn't matter that the castle was cold.

She expected it, but Big-O didn't tear her clothes and ravish her. Underneath the portrait on the wall of a great big hydra rearing its head in attack pose, he let her close her eyes on a memory foam pillow that understood her head.

In the morning, she stared at the first mirror she'd ever studied. The house was full of mirrors, but she looked at the arched wall mirror with bohemian frills gilded in gold in Big-O's bedroom. She studied her midnight skin, half-petal mouth, a natural cherry ripe. Strong cheekbones, the hint of a dimple. Line-thin brows, full-lashed eyes. They were scrutiny eyes that attacked before one could harm what was inside. Searing pupils that danced orange flames.

Big-O sees the shimmer at the third quarter of the match. It has calves and ankles, a sparkle of face that comes and goes. It's a giant monstrosity that's also a beauty right there behind the posts. The sighting comes with a ringing in his head that's like the approach of a blast, or the aftermath of it.

He positions, but the dazzle in his eyes... His mind is boggled. He knows the kick isn't right way before the ball leaves his boot.

The crowd groans.

The other team's player rushes the ball out. Another intent on a tackle makes good of it. Now it's Big-O's coach banging on. A momentum player whips the ball even further away. Another of the team gets a mark in the middle of a pack.

Gee, they make hard work of it!

It's not pretty, but they just keep at it!

The other team's ball sails home on their side.

The tackle! The reward! The finish!

Pure beauty!

Centre bounce, ball goes the other side's way. Another goal, then another.

That's a big comeback!

Parks his name in front of the sticks!

The ball's in motion the length of the ground. A shimmy, Big-O's.

He sprints with the ball, finds a body. A smother off his boot, but King Charlie dives on it, hooks one between the posts.

He sneaks one home! Perhaps there's hope.

Does he love it! Oh, yes, he does!

But that's about it, starkness on the scoreboard. King Charlie cleans up a fumble. It's grubby play out and out. A bad time for Big-O to lose his feet, no ball shaping on his boot to split the middle of the posts.

It's an off day for our champ!

His goal-kicking's deserted him!

Someone kicks the ball underneath Big-O's legs—another goal for the other team.

"Waiting for griffins to come home?" yells Big-O's coach.

"Mate?" says King Charlie. He's holding Big-O's jumper. "Thought you were an A-grader—fog's happening?"

"I dipped," says Big-O.

"No more dipping."

But shimmer has consumed him. Big-O feels burnt inside out. His aim is more a blemish than a kick.

Coach is giving instructions for the bench. Big-O complies, doesn't mean he can't beg.

"Get me back there, I've got this."

"That won't be a vibe."

"Please! Coach."

"I don't give a fog how good you are. Just no."

And Big-O sits out the match, a ball of black smoke in his head.

"That's it," spits King Charlie in the locker room. "Do that again, and I'll hate you all the way."

"Dude—"

"Pre-empt the hate."

Fontasia's never seen Big-O like this after a match. His body language shows deep hurt. He's gaunt, sallow. He falls back when she reaches to touch him—he's never been crazy on sex—but this!

He climbs between the sheets, pulls a doona over his head. It's her turn to stroke his all-over crew cut, bedraggled. She notices with astonishment a dance of light on her arm. It's more like a flicker, what you might see when you light a match in the dark.

He closes his eyes, snores to her stroking.

She looks at herself in the arched wall mirror with its bohemian frills. The scrutiny in her eyes has softened. Her midnight skin is more alive than ever. And there's a halo on her head. She feels... half-god.

The gang swings by at dawn to collect him for practice.

"What's with the heating?" says Boak.

"Mate—don't act like you haven't been," says King Charlie.

"Jack 'er up," says Norton.

They sit in vintage high-backed chairs carved with baby griffins. They talk, sip tea, eat wattleseed biscuits in the castle with tiered pendants and chandeliers in raindrop cascade.

King Charlie looks up the winding staircase—its fading faces and headless busts—and speaks his mind. "Where's the big guy?"

Fontasia knows where the big guy is: bunched into a ball on the chrome-studded king bed, won't turn from the wall. She says nothing.

King Charlie cups his hands. "Push the demon out," he shouts.

"Push 'er 'ard," says Norton.

"Harder," says Boak. Tosses his dreadlocks as if to make the point.

The cleaner does come in once a week. First time the doorbell rang, Fontasia answered, it was the cleaner with his duster, bucket, spray mop. He peered at her, wondering at her presence. He was a looker she could well date, she thought. She looked at his tools. "I carry everything," he said, as if that explained it.

Now Fontasia watches him from the window clipping the hedge. A stir behind—she's surprised to see Big-O summon the legs to climb out of bed.

She goes to the match with him. But the outcome is fiercely bad. The other team gets involved early. Their key player makes a surge from the onset to an early opening goal.

Then another, drilled directly in front of the posts.

Before the other team can line up another laser, King Charlie, Norton and Boak put up a fight. A floater misses the goal.

Can't keep it in!

They're not going quiet!

An offensive avalanche. A poke in the eye happens, as does a goal for the other team.

That's inspiration!

A big scalping!

"The shimmer," mutters Big-O in the limo all the way home. "It was waiting. All the time behind the posts."

The gang comes to take him out for a cheer. He shakes his head. They look at him like a stranger. He's faded, more exoskeleton than skin.

"Since when didn't you like clubbing?" asks King Charlie.

"Give 'er a go," says Norton.

"Mate?" says Boak.

"I'll go," says Fontasia.

She feels better than she's ever felt. Stares at her reflection in the mirror as she gets ready, pulls on a tiny dress full of swing. She contemplates the halo on her head.

"There's a glow on you," says King Charlie.

"Yer look insane!" agrees Norton.

They ride to a bouncy place with a neon sign that says Opium Poppy. It's a blend of modern, bar and party, living-room mode in places. Purple strobe lighting vacillates with lime, flickering to the beat that's a proper *DOOF! DOOF!*

The place is crawling with nude women and pimps, all clearly injected. No shame doing caps—luminescent pills exchange hands. Someone's likely doing a line in the toilet. The retro music is full of love, Shazam and dynamite. Hues and kinetics.

"Do you have bud?" a drunkard slurs in her face. He pongs like he's gobbled squirrel fish with black garlic. She turns from him.

"Dance?" it's Boak, right in her face too. And it's erotic.

Fontasia looks around, as if for permission. From whom? Norton is nowhere in sight—Fontasia hopes he's not doing billies, or he'll flunk the drug test. King Charlie is downing magi-coloured shots. At least he's not rolling.

"That won't be an appletini," says Boak. He tosses his dreads. "Nothing fruity or frozen here. You wanna dance or wot?"

She opens herself to the rhythm, his rhythm. His body flows like water. She throws her arms and floats to the flickering light.

Later, he buys her an old fashioned: sugar lump, water, ice cube, bitters, whiskey, lemon peel.

"Maybe I prefer a dark and stormy," she says to his ear.

"What?" The music so loud.

"A dark... oh, never mind."

"What?"

"Rum!"

"Deeply same."

Norton's bouncing up the walls. He volleys all jacked up into this pack. "Wot's up, cuz. Wot you lookin' at?" Starts a fight because (1) they're not his cousins and (2) what they're looking at is none of his foggin' mind. King Charlie falls in, so it's eight to two.

Boak tosses his dreads, "Foggity," and leaps with a landing fist.

Of course, they get bounced. Tossed out to the curb.

"Thrive in packs like hyenas," spits Boak at the bouncers.

"Hey, I'm lit," laughs Norton.

"Tell big boy he should be a sparkie or a chippie if he can't kick a ball," says King Charlie, as they drop her off. "What do you reckon?" There's worry on his face.

"Something's happening," says Fontasia. She can't imagine Big-O as an electrician or a carpenter. Like ever.

"It's a dimension," laughs Norton. He waves his hands in a spooky way.

As she steps gingerly into the castle, fumbles with keys, cusses, Fontasia can't remember who was driving.

"Night good?" croaks Big-O inside covers.

"Off the charts," says Fontasia. "Insanely good."

"Someone get decked?"

She breaks into a grin. "Good as."

Big-O doesn't know how he does it, because he's dizzy all the time, depressed too. But he spruces up for the next match. Perhaps it's the thought of Fontasia having fun with his mates, him missing out. It pulls the cast from his knees, cracks open the tomb.

"Remember the hate?" says King Charlie. "Love you loads, but I've got a life. Play to the death."

"Gotta show me face tomorrow," says Norton.

"Damn right," says Boak.

But there's no curler. The ball swings away from the posts.

An off night for our fav.

Nothing he touches is gold.

The other team's wingspan is in the smallest forward. Aarts. Number 8. He floats one, hair in all directions.

It's a beautiful strike!

Spectacularly good!

The other team's belief is growing. Someone committed to a smother gets it right.

It's as if Big-O's playing to chance. He puts his head down, kicks a doozie across the goal face where the shimmer is watching.

Brutalised!

It's a bummer!

Big-O's knee is sore. His whole body hurts. More so, his eyes.

At the third quarter, he tries to start something. The other team drowns it. He passes to King Charlie, to Norton, to Boak—can't find a way forward. A gang tackle splays the ball towards the boundary line. The crowd groans on the seats.

It's a mess on the field. Big-O's under siege, zero on his board. He looks at the clock, an eternity left. A less fast player overtakes Big-O's feet—he loses ball possession. When he gets it back, he kicks wide. Someone knocks him down, takes his calf.

Big-O's clutching at his leg. King Charlie runs towards him. "Mate? Foggity fog. Be alright." He stokes Big-O's hair. "Doc will be here in a sec."

Boak, Norton, sphere him from the crowd.

This fight is done, says the commentator.

That's a scalping!

Big-O's coach spits on the ground.

She orders Uber Eats from his favourite joint, d'Angelo's. The pizza's slathered in a rich cream of ricotta in pesto broccoli. She strokes his crew cut as he picks at the crust, head still on a pillow. He tells her about a blinding light that deconstructs his essence, how he regrets his life, questions his existence.

He declines to touch a morsel, looks at her with wounded eyes. "I don't get it," he says, then blacks out. He's dizzy all the time, muttering nonsense, before the blackouts.

His friends carry him, visit the icy castle when they can.

"And the heating, man!" says Boak.

"Jack 'er up," says Norton.

Fontasia shows them up the windy staircase to where Big-O's roped in sheets like a mummy, careened into shadow.

"The shimmer—" he croaks weakly. "Big bird."

"Shoot 'er in the head," says Norton.

"That's a lot of fucking bullets," says Boak.

"It's about the margin," says King Charlie.

"Nah. Point blank range," says Norton.

They don't tell Big-O that Coach went feral about him, had to make tough decisions.

Fontasia can't drive the limo. She takes an Uber to the city, watches the barista etch a kangaroo paw on the froth of her latte. He picks her from the queue. 'You the hot one?'

The flower is gold velvet. She lingers the sips. Each nut and smoke, bitter and flower, consoles her from a fading that's a wrong turn. She knows how she likes her coffee: extra hot.

She steps back into the castle's freeze, returns to a ghostly shroud on the bed.

She looks at the mirror: her whole body is shimmering. She feels indomitable. Supremely happy. Finally home.

The doorbell—it's the cleaner. She flicks him off with a fat tip, asks him to come back next week. She takes possession, makes a mental note to sort out the heating. She sizes up the pantry. Pasta in ribbons, spirals, tubes and hair-thins. Flour, sugar, canned tomatoes, unopened oyster sauce.

She has no clue what the hell to cook.

But

  she'll

    cook.

Nyamizi, the Skinless One

RAIN CASCADES to the rhythm of drums in her head. Its wet invitation washes Nyamizi for the role she was born into—setting aside all the traditions of the Moon Goddess. She understands that she's half-breed, and one side is winning in her core. Without guidance from her mother, right now is about dancing with the sky, emptying her soul of itself until she feels nothing but the joy of giving—even when it means swaying in the rain and chanting farewell to all Nyamizi knows.

She thinks of her mother, the music warrior.

A crescendo of beats on downturned calabashes and pots faded to where no one saw.

"Again, *mazi*," begged Nyamizi. "Please play the beats."

"Tomorrow, I promise," said Pili. "For tonight you must sleep." A cough tickled her chest. Today, there was blood.

She put away the pots, lined the calabashes along the wall near the three-stone hearth. Tucked Nyamizi with a leopard skin and watched her bout with sleep until it conquered her. She continued to watch her daughter purr lightly on the soft grass bed inside the darkened cave.

Pili took the opportunity of silence—not that the child irked, but she was a curious one full of questions—to ponder life. And death. She smiled wryly.

Inside was inside, yet outside was everywhere in a forbidden love that transitioned to nowhere in a sleeping cave. Many years ago, she'd kept lanterns burning, but darkness was a surety despite her visitor who brought gifts of goat milk, yams, cassava, mangoes, a dangle of rabbits tied to a pole, millet wine and sorghum beer. It didn't take long for Pili and her visitor to know the moment when a strange amity became something else, along with a race of pulse, a linger of touch. Smell became sentiment, and the aroma of kudu lily and devil's thorn entered with the woman who was an enemy and a friend to Pili and all she knew.

Her name was Sumba, a daughter of Sorghum... She touched Pili like a lucky bean creeper. One dusk, Sumba walked barefoot as before into the cave, but this time put her face near Pili's lips, cupped her chin and became a lover. It was a touch that was a melt, or perhaps it was Pili who melted—lit by countless sunlights that fell to an eon of winters when Sumba left.

Yes, inside was inside, no matter the womb of time. The tale was the same, just a little different now. A mother's love for her daughter was its own ilk. Nyamizi had no skin and her eyes were white—unlike lush-haired Sumba whose skin was alive with the colour of mud. Perhaps it was a whisper of ghosts in Nyamizi's hair that made it yellow, and Pili understood that they told the child about birth and death, and everything in-between that goats, giants and goblins knew. Outside had foes. Demons attacking every which way in a forever war.

It was no secret that Nyamizi saw them in her dreams. It worried Pili to see the child fret in her sleep, until she snapped to, sat up with her cry of alarm. "*Mazi!*"

"Hush, my child."

"Are they real?"

"Demons? I can't tell about the ones you see, *oponzi*, dear child."

"Why are we outcasts?"

"*Yo mbago*, I love you—this you must know. Although I have raised you in a hole and feel that you're sinking towards dark water in your dreams. You already know you're half and half. Hybrid. Metztli the Moon Goddess doesn't like this."

"What about the demons?"

"What about them, child?"

"Do they care about outcasts?"

"I would have hoped for a care of nurture, but I think not."

"And why so, mother?"

"I am the vessel that swallowed echoes and lifeseed from a daughter of Eshe. The Moon Goddess and the spellcaster are unhappy with this."

And is that a mind?

That is no mind to me, my child.

For why, mazi?

Because your heart, oponzi, dear child, is the sweet flower upon tugging waves.

It went on... The child's curiosity endless, silenced for a moment with a yearning. "Hum me a song, *mazi*."

"Let me find you a story of the Eternal Realm and tell you why, with those eyes, you are a fire watcher."

Nyamizi is good with the arrow, bending the *vushale* just right before release. She's now perfect with a spear, but wonders if her weapons are enough to keep away an army of demons. Her mother did best to prepare her for the outside world. Stepping out of the cave, Nyamizi hadn't expected it to be surrounded by the worlds of her mother's stories. Tall palm trees with shiny leaves pregnant with water. Golden sand that warms toes. God-perfect waters filled with memory. That perfection is the world of the holy city, not here.

Outside is worse than Nyamizi expected. It's dark and wet and full of smells. It's a horrible place to die, especially alone. After a night of following the sound of rain, she succumbs to sleep. There, her dreams become flesh, take on faces of long-haired warriors battling ruby-eyed beasts far older than time. Nyamizi stands, entranced, white-eyed and watching: litheness and leanness, speed and muscle, atop a sacred mountain in the distance. She beholds the beauty of war, the longing to guard and protect in a clink of swords, a whizz of arrows that look you in the eye and make widows and orphans.

On one hand, sight of the bloodied knoll puts fear in her stomach—the kind of terror that clutches, then claws. On the other it's a call. Valour is curled inside her fear. Nyamizi has a calling to be there, near the horizon, close to the mountain peak. It's a long way, but it calls to her.

She falls out of sleep in panic or worry that the dream will never take her hand and guide her through shadows. It'll never walk her safely across the one and only road—this dark and wet one—that brings the fulfilment of her quest nearer. It's a fulfilment she's been hunting way before she knew she was looking.

The light in her head speaks words she must heed. They signal she must protect the realm of realms.

"*Mazi*, tell me about Sumba."

"Again?"

"I want to hear it."

"It was a war like no other. The An'Fre were winning and my people of the island, the Otomi, were pulling back, still fighting. I felt eyes from a distance. I looked and my instinct was right—how could she see me through my special shield of invisibility? But she did. She was a gifted one of An'Fre who pierced my magic with her spear. Did you know that a leaping blow from the leg of an ostrich can kill a lion?"

"I know, *mazi*."

Pili's shoulders shook with a new spurt of coughing that was like the grunt of a wild cat. She paused, then continued: "The warrior rode a monster ostrich, toppled me from my yellow-eyed lion and his flowing mane. You know the rest."

"No. Tell it, *mazi*."

"When Sumba's spear tore through my shield, it also pierced my rib. She galloped back and stood with her giant bird on my lion, the gold in his mane now clumped with blood. She leaned towards my face and there was something in her face..."

"What was it?"

"Patience, my child or you'll have to tell the story yourself. I've told it more than the count of stars. How are you still curious to hear it?"

"But I am."

"Sumba pulled out the spear and the pain of the shaft coming out was worse than a sheaf of spears going in. I let out a cry and plummeted to blackness."

"And then what?"

"Light came back inside the blackness, and it was a shine not from the sun, but the beauty of the murdering one of An'Fre whose ostrich had felled my lion. The one who had pierced me at speed with a spear and slowly pulled it out. We were inside a cave, my torso wrapped in herbs and bark."

"What did you do?"

"I asked her: 'How did you see me?' She said, 'Your magic called to my twilight essence.' I asked: 'Why did you save me?' She said, 'Perhaps it was something to do with the Spell of Making.' I did not understand then, until you, *oponzi*, came along."

"But why did Sumba leave?"

"She saw you, a child of darkness, born without skin, and thought she understood her curse. I tried to tell her your difference was a blessing, but she feared it was a punishment from the gods she had displeased by contaminating the bloodline."

"Oh! *Mazi*."

"Mine is a wound that never healed. It nearly killed me when she left us."

"I want to be a Sorghum child."

"You're a dreamer and a bit of a story yourself—" A spurt of new coughing swallowed Pili's words.

"You're cold, *mazi*. Look, I saved this for you." Nyamizi held out a piece of cold coal from the hearth. It began to glow as she held it.

It warmed the cave, and Pili's coughing settled. "You have a gift, *oponzi*."

"I don't know—"

"Isn't it wonderful to hope that the ancestors will take you in their care?"

"The ancestors of the Otomi, or the ones of An'Fre?"

"You have claim to both."

Rain has settled. Nyamizi rises in the orange-brown of the night and moves with unwillingness from the shelter of a wind-chiselled boulder filled with holes that perhaps spy for the gods. Wind blows like a ghost, reminding her to forget the shelter of the cave in the old world from which she emerged.

She thinks of her mother who told stories of the first daughters of An'Fre, whose music with upturned pots and calabashes told of an ostrich-riding warrior who stole hearts.

She feels a deep and terrible sadness.

"You must go now, child."

"To the Otomi? I will get help, I promise!"

"Those ones will kill you. You're marked different—even rubbing charcoal is not escaping that lack of skin."

"Then where can I find help for you, *mazi*?"

"You have more hope with the An'Fre. Sumba showed me this with her kindness."

"But I don't speak the language!"

"Yours is a universal tongue. You're young and pure. Gifted with the essence of the All-Mother."

"But what can I do when I get there, if I reach there? A place I don't know."

"Find your mother."

"It's you, *mazi*!"

"Find your other mother. Follow the water, go west and keep west until you see the peak of a mountain. It's Mount Jaleh. You must climb it because at its peak is a village named Marduri. That's where the An'Fre live. It's where you'll find Sumba."

"I don't want to leave you."

"I should have let you wander, but I feared the harm demons might do you. You'll hunch into yourself inside this crippling cave. It's my time, and yours to know your destiny. I want you to touch me with an ember."

"Wait. What?"

"But you must, dear one. My smoke will rise—the gods know I've paid my dues in full in this wretched cave. I've not stolen a moment's laughter. Tonight, I shall sit on the right side of the Moon Goddess."

"No, *mazi*!"

It's the hardest thing to touch your own mother with an ember, and see the lift of her brow as she lights and gives herself to the Moon Goddess.

Nyamizi called for her mother's return, over and over, until she was too hungry to sit crying and alone in the cave.

But goblins—yellow and green and carnivorous all the way west to the cold mountain—were hungry too, and Nyamizi's spears and arrows were not enough. She breathed her last—or so she thought—surrounded by an army of beasts leaping to finish her. A godmother of goblins bared bad teeth and a reek Nyamizi would never forget. She closed her eyes, touched the coal inside her hem and prayed that, despite a ripping death, her two lines of ancestry would guide her spirit to meet her *mazi*.

She opened her eyes at a bellow, and was astonished to see the ember aglow and the goblin aflame. The fire that shot from her eyes incinerated the rest of the goblins and all that was left was soot.

Perhaps I too am a Sorghum child, she mused, as she ran, harder and faster through jungle towards Mount Jaleh whose peak was now showing. She doubted a little when she reached the rumble of the cold mountain and saw flames rise from its lip in the distance. But she climbed it, hands and knees, rocks and rugged terrain that cut. She doubted a lot as she reached a village of huts at the peak, and the An'Fre tumbled out of their huts. Children took one look at her lack of skin and fell back in bewilderment.

Then warrior girls with long spears, poison-tipped arrows and *vushale* like Nyamizi's surrounded her, tensed and braced for attack. Nyamizi's fists clenched. She felt her eyes begin to glow. Her feet left the ground of their own accord. She saw fear in the ones circling her levitation.

A tall warrior, rippling muscles in her lean arms and torso, stepped forward with boldness in her chin. "What are you?"

"I am An'Fre."

The others laughed nervously, but not this one.

"And Otomi."

The others gasped, then parted as an elder in gilded robes and a billow of white hair, her ancient face wearing eyes of wisdom, approached. "Enough. Namazzi! I will take it from here."

"All-Mother." Namazzi bowed and stepped back.

"Mmhhh," said All-Mother. She studied Nyamizi and her levitation.

"I see you have hidden powers, but it's ill manners to hover. Why don't you come down?"

Nyamizi fell to the ground, suddenly tired, hungry but unafraid.

All-Mother touched Nyamizi's chin to lift her face. "I knew my daughters were wilful—just not this much. You have her face."

She straightened and swept her eyes across the An-Fre. "Don't just stand there and gawp. Find this wretched one some food." She turned to Nyamizi. "And you, child. What can I do for you?"

Nyamizi climbed to her feet, head bowed.

"I want to fight and protect Ngolo Ade, the holy city."

"Mmhhh. And right now?"

"I want to see my mother." She looked at the elder.

"Mmhhh." All-Mother clicked her tongue. "It was Sumba's fate to be a warrior, not a maker. I see now why she faded. How she displeased us all."

"Please, she's all I have now. Take me to her."

"*Umozi*, no one tampers with the Spell of Making, sullies the bloodline, and lives. But I see the essence in you. I welcome you, lost Sorghum child. Now you have found us."

"Yes, All-Mother."

"Come," she smiled and took Nyamizi's hand. "Let me tell you more about Ngolo Ade."

A Visit to Lamont

OVERNIGHT PETAL misplaces her voice—the normal one. What remains is hums, barks and grunts. Her face is a mask: cold, forgotten. She's trapped in someplace only belief can restore.

But Acha is not a man of faith. Prayer is no option. He does Easter eggs—truffles mostly, boozy ones with real gin, whiskey, Baileys or Kahlua. And Christmas cake, drowned in spiced rum and amaretto. Who gives a hoot about orange, ginger or burnt sugar? He once saw the casting out of demons in a church years ago when he was little—it was enough to make him love snakes. Other than that...

Now he contemplates visiting a pastor or a priest, especially when he sees Petal fall in throes on the carpet, bluster in tongues. Her words sound like *exsecratus, execrabilis, maudite, sacré, jinni, shetani.* She drools and foams.

Acha steals into the kitchen for its solitude. A lone fan whirs overhead this tepid summer night. He uses his smart phone to search online for the meaning of Petal's chants, or their likeness. He's perturbed by what he finds. Daemons, beasts, fiends... That's why he needs a church. Or a graveyard.

What worries happens as they sleep. He wakes at intervals to find Petal looking at him from upside down on the ceiling like a giant bat. One time he leaps with a cry, takes the car keys. But no, he doesn't want to leave and return home to the wind that's tearing her stockings, her skin, and all that.

He looks at recent events and thinks about how the whole damned thing happened.

It was bloody hot. Everyone got the memo because everyone was at Lamont Winery that sun-scorched afternoon. Vans, saloon cars, four-wheel drives... all squeezed into a dusty car park facing the vineyard. Dogs barked, loped tongues out across the fields. They crashed into restaurant tables as children chortled, knocked about, some near a tasting table with its dirty-mouthed man and a sign that read: Free sampling 2–3pm.

It was an escape from being cooped up in the townhouse in Brookdale, off Powell Crescent—even if it was four-bedroomed, tiled-floored, had a patio and a workshop. It made sense to take the rental when he and Petal moved in together.

"Easy care gardens, love it," said Petal.

"Large kitchen, love it," said Acha. "Close to schools, shops, public transport."

"You've got a car—what do we need public transport for? And schools? Bloke, we haven't talked about kids yet. That's a bit rushing, no?"

Acha was the broody type, unwilling to commit to an argument. And this house was better than the share-pad he lived in with his cousin Lumumba who drove a lime car that was small, an island with its number plate: PONY4ME.

Lumumba fell in love with the edge of things. He taught Acha to loosen up.

"The best way to tumble-turn in a pool," said Lumumba, "is with your face relaxed. You approach the wall at speed, flip. You push off the wall, your face at ease. Listen to the water's whispers as you surge, breathe out through the nose and your lungs are good for another go with your lips."

"Toying with death," said Acha. "I can hold my breath twenty-five seconds max. Once water gets in, it takes four, maybe six minutes to die."

"Loosen up, cuz. Make tomorrow a shore."

Now at the winery, Petal bee-lined for the tasting table with its dirty-mouthed man. "They warned me at the bar," she laughed. "Said he's

Chye's husband, owns the joint. Was it the dress?" Petal swirled in her bohemian flow. "What damage did they think I could do? All the time Chye was right there, behind the bar. She said, 'Laugh at his jokes, or give it back to him.'"

Acha was fine to chill under an umbrella table, take in the scenery. He'd seen potty-mouthed bastards, like this one with his beer gut and ponytail. He was cracking jokes, oblivious to the discomfiture of customers.

"This is a chardonnay, new release. That's a young cab sauv blend. I was managing a bunch of backpackers picking grapes for hourly pay. I said to one—she was from Zimbabwe or something: 'What's your name, honey?' She said, 'Uvuvwevwevwe.' I said, 'Right. What happened on your way here?' She said, 'I was on a V/Line bus that hit a kangaroo.' I said, 'You murdered a bloody roo. Fine. None of that Uvuvuvu. Your name's Killer.'"

Petal laughed. "That's so racist. What wine is this?"

Potty-mouth said, "Yummy. So tasty, you want to throw it on yourself and lick it off, so you don't have to share it."

Acha approached, spoke in low tones to Petal's ear. "You want me to defend you?"

"Feminism. I can handle this jerk."

Acha walked back to the umbrella, as Potty-mouth was saying: "Here we have fortified wine. Please, turn around."

"Why?" said Petal.

"I don't like to watch a woman enjoying herself."

"You're grounded for a week."

"Fucken hell. Let me get my guns and show you how grounded I am."

The banter irked Acha, perhaps more that Petal was unperturbed by it. But a black cat with bottle green eyes was meowing, persistent, at his feet. The sound echoed dark colours: deep red, dark brown, purple, charcoal and bursts of shadow. The meows commanded centre stage, rough to ignore.

He looked around: surrounded by people talking, laughing, shouting. Yet this cat from nowhere... At first he thought the sound was pitiful. It reminded him of the forlorn cry of a sick or tired baby. Maybe the *aaah, waah, gaah* of a bird at the crack of dawn. Now he was sure its perseverance was angry.

The air wobbled. He looked away one minute, and a woman with smoky-green eyes stood where the cat had been. She was dressed in a gunny sack. Something woven, hessian jute—the kind of material one might use to ship wool or put coffee in so it could breathe.

He blinked and the burlap sack woman was everywhere: at that table, behind the bar, inside the restaurant, on the vineyard. Keep cool, don't make a scene, he said to himself. But she multiplied, doubled in numbers each time he looked. Now she was plucking at her hemp by the flowerbeds on the way to the outdoor toilets. She did it in a way that reminded Acha of tomorrow.

Petal and Potty-mouth were still at it. He was leaning close to her bosom, saying, "Can I ask you a personal question?"

"Shoot."

"Have you experienced a white monster?'"

"A black one is bigger."

"You dirty bitch. I was talking about wine."

"Bastard. I was talking about port."

Now the burlap sack woman sat opposite Acha. She nodded at Petal and Potty-mouth. "You enjoying that?"

"It's harmless fun."

"Not for Chye, it isn't."

"What are you? Her godmother?"

"Maybe."

"Always blame the woman. What about the man?"

"Who knows? Might wake up, find himself in a cage."

Acha rose, suddenly incensed. He matched to the tasting table, snatched Petal by the arm.

"What?" she said.

"We're done here."

"But the food inside the restaurant—" She broke mid-sentence. Her sea-blue gaze held the burlap sack woman's smoky-green one, as if in startlement. Then she spoke in a small voice: "Yes, let's go home," as if enchanted.

She was quiet all the way back to Brookdale, staring through the windscreen.

He starts dialling 000 then thinks about it. A black man with a dead white woman in his house. A rattle: she's breathing. Eyes rolled back in the head. He lays her medication like the Milky Way: spiral with a hazy connection. Gobblers, puffers, sprayers—mostly antihistamines, ethical nutrients, vitamins, laxatives, mild things for aches and sprains, all on the kitchen table. Nothing measures to the scale of Uranus. If men are from Mars, some understand plenty to open a curled fist. He opens his fist and traces a finger inside his palm to study a reading of the moon, lanterns, boats, birds, and a telescope to Pluto calmly out of focus. Women are from Pluto.

Dusk slips in like any other night. Yellow light streams into the room. A nightjar scrapes out yonder, then a soft *tyeow* as it calls. An overhead fan hums its icy draft. The evening news flickers on TV: A coalition blunder. A woman caught reading Rushdie while driving. A monarch dead at 99. Tech, viral variants, data leaks, a military coup.

There's a method to Petal's madness. She flares every four hours, then dies. The mask slips back on her face, dusk. He needs a grimoire, a textbook of magic to undo the hex. He knows enough about a hex to know when one's been placed. Where in the city does he find cowrie shells? The skin of a black mamba? A hyena's tooth? He'd love to get hands on an ostrich's tail. Might he swap all those things—unfindable here—with mead? Manuka honey? An emu's poo? Outside, the melody of a nightjar calling, calling.

Rain.

He sleeps poorly in the roar of thunder.

Then he's got the runs—he thought his stomach could take anything: Locusts. Plucked mangoes fresh from a tree. Tape worms. Bilharzia. No. His toilet is yellow water. He feels dizzy, a churn in his gut. He steps back into the bedroom as Petal falls in shakes, eyes, head and body turned in his direction. He wonders if he should try and contain her convulsions.

He calls Lumumba.

Trust is metal with no price guide. Belief is a track set to squares and keys—it's about positioning your finger on a keyboard and feeling nothing but QWERTY. Space bar ZXCV. Each keystroke loosens your body to forget hardness. Your mind becomes a floating feather the size of molten rain. You look at the screen with the words of your language in SDFG. Each key, num lock, shift up down, demands feeding between leg stretches and tea breaks as a flat laminate and layers of circuitry buried in the surface converse in binary. Billions of transistors brace for ZXCV and belief, hidden in 1s and 0s.

"Put socks between her teeth so she doesn't bite off her tongue," says Lumumba.

"Socks?"

"I don't know—a wooden spoon?"

"Cuz, despite what you've heard, it's impossible to swallow your tongue and choke."

"If you fucking know this much about convulsions, the fuck are you waking me up at midnight for?"

"The burlap sack woman."

"You need burlap string for the hexagon. Thirteen candles in a circle, and a spotless black hen."

"Seriously, cuz?"

"Heirloom Pure—"

"Where the fog do I get burlap string?"

"Acha, if all you got from this convo is the string, you're stuffed. Try Yarns on Collie, Crossways Wool & Fabrics, even eBay."

"What?"

"Or a charity shop."

Acha shakes his head. "You're Perth-born, cuz. Where do you get this juju nonsense?"

But Petal heaved a sigh of death and stopped breathing, and Acha knew he would do anything his dual major in engineering and physics hadn't taught him. After all, he'd come to Australia, and the best he could do with Université de Lubumbashi was drive an Uber. The university was one of the largest in the Democratic Republic of Congo—he did sessional teaching. But he still lived east in the slums of Kinshasa, riding a bicycle daily to work along the Ndjili River... until his Australian-born cousin Lumumba—son of Auntie Upendo and her white husband—

sponsored his migration. Lumumba, with his pale skin and McDreamy eyes, had secured his own IT job in government with simply a diploma from a polytechnic.

Acha thought school learning taught him language, but it was broken. He needs to become the scientist he'd abandoned. He needs to work through unseen forces, to rediscover *dada*, *nyoka*, *mbuzi* and fragments of the dialect of Africa he's taken for granted. He's in a world that has made tradition useless yet it scrapes up debt, materialism, egotism. A family of two is more than plentiful, because choice banishes children and forces legs up corporate ladders—like it did Upendo and her husband. Society is a metonym for socialism, where it makes sense to agree to disagree on dog-eat-dog, and me-myself-and-I. Psychotherapists, never mystics, prescribe pills, more pills, for the dust that is human. Until someone discovers the hidden element of stopping the pill-swallowing and loving other people. That's the cure.

He loves Petal, and feels a deep and terrible sadness. The spirit of lament in his core makes certain he'll seek the black hen or cockerel. A search engine gives him the location of farms that sell the black Australorp. But nothing gives at Poultry and Birds in Midvale. The Pet Grocer in Ascot is a waste of time. Swan Valley Birds, even Birds 'N All are useless.

The black hen springs from a private sale. It's a home in Banjup, a suburb of Perth within the City of Cockburn. He drives past rural residential properties, plant nurseries and hobby farms, before he reaches the house with its roaming goat that cocks its head and looks at him with one blue eye, one brown one. Its shrewd eyes remind him of his grandmother, long passed.

He's considering a goat horn, or a goat sacrifice, when the owner, Chad, dissuades him from it. He says, "Eight-hundred dollars for a whole goat, I'm not selling."

They walk past piglets huddled together. A sow is squealing and grunting, wallowing in a nearby trough of mud. Acha contemplates an ewe—nursing two pure-white lambs. Sweet-eyed, perky eared. He tries not to think of them as dinner, reminds himself that what he needs is black.

They reach an outdoor aviary with a perch that holds a falcon. Another has cerulean birds, Columbidae, finches. There's an emu—a docile thing with golden brown eyes. She's two metres tall, shaggy grey hairs on her blue-black neck. She grunts, pig-like, at Acha, then booms. Soft fluffy feathers on her body rise and he moves away.

They arrive at a walk-in chicken run.

"Grow to a healthy weight of 8.5 pounds, 6–10 years," Chad is saying. "You're lucky if you get an egg a day—I'd average it to four or five eggs a week."

"How much?"

"Fifty bucks for a five-month-old near the point of laying. One-twenty for a trio—two hens and a cockerel."

"All black?"

"Shit no."

A black rooster, a tuft of feathers on its head, comes running. It's squawking for dear life, leaps into Acha as if it knows him. "I'll take this black one here."

"Odd," says Chad. Scratches his head. "Can't remember that one—think I'd know it with that crest."

At Bunnings, Acha leaves the rooster raising hell in the Uber's boot. He finds saws, trimmers, wire strippers, folding knives, craft knives, pocket knives—nothing he's looking for. The Knives and Tools comes close but the best is Tentworld, who call themselves the camping experts. He gets a gator machete on special for $69.99.

"How the heck do I do that?"

"Fuck, I don't know. Just chant something," says Lumumba.

They've sneaked at dusk to Lamont Winery, dead weight between them in Petal. Acha is afraid they'll be caught—stupid chook won't shut the hell up.

"Like call on the goddess of fire to feed the flame," Lumumba is saying. "And if the candles go out—"

"It means the goddess has accepted my request."

"Cuz. If the candles go out, mate you're fucked. Stand in the circle and chant."

"Chant *what* in the godawful din with this bloody chook?"

"Something like *I want you to break the harm upon this woman. Take my gift, oh sweet goddess.* Man, get balls, just pull out some shit!"

Acha closes his eyes and rocks inside the circle.

"Take my gift." Louder. "TAKE MY GIFT." Nothing happens. "Bright flame, light of mine... This is bullshit!"

"Good. Keep trying."

"How's this:

Goddess bright
Give me what I ask
A little healing on this black night
Bring Petal back from her curse."

Petal is in rigor mortis on the grass inside the circle, her pale face all blue.

"Good one," says Lumumba. "Don't forget the cockerel."

Acha holds the chook by the legs as it squawks, swings the machete.

"The fuck, cuz! You could have got my dick!"

"I can't slice the throat," says Acha. "I *won't*."

"Be a girl."

"What if I don't get the jugular?"

"I don't know—you're the one born in Lubumbashi. They slaughter chickens all the time."

Acha closes his eyes. He allows himself to feel. He remembers ancestry, his grandmother and her goat eyes. The way she chewed dried tobacco and spat it—brown globules rich and earthy like wet hay. Once she let him taste a fresh leaf. It reminded him of grass: sharp, full of spice. A bit like peppered soil sprinkled with the dust of smoked wood.

He opens his eyes, takes a deep breath. He lays the potbellied cockerel on the ground: breast down, head facing away, beak side down. It turns its head. He notices a band holding the crest of feathers like a ponytail on its head. The bird looks at him with a plea and a pitiful squawk. Something fleeting in its eye... He shakes his head, lifts the machete, closes his eyes. Somewhere in the distance, the persistent meow of a cat.

Acha opens his eyes and looks at Petal. Her head is jerking. Then she sits up straight and stares at something that isn't there. Slowly her eyes gain focus.

She looks at Acha, then Lumumba, and finally the beheaded cockerel.

"You kinky dawg," she says. "We on a threesome, or something, no?"

Industrial Pleasure

The Demand

MAYASA has had it. She's far too long been scouring ovens, wiping racks, shelving pots, chucking contaminated food prep containers, handling chefs who are sour over their precious knives, non-stick pans. As if that's all. The restaurant is just one gig. There are the toilets: her hands wrist-deep scrubbing faeces from the throne with a brush, then the sound of falling water. Folding napkins. Arranging shampoos, body wash, lotions that claim to be organic, but really aren't—the best you get is beeswax, almond oil, maybe goat milk. And what about the hotel rooms? Emptying waste baskets—heaven forbid, you don't want to know the things moneyed people chuck. Once she found a laptop. Sure, it was broken, but still!

Mayasa is done pushing trolleys spilling with pleated towels, lining tissues, placing beer, wine and baby bottles of still water in mini-refrigerators. Fluffing goose-feather pillows that hold too many secrets of murdered memories. Her incomings seriously undermine her outgoings, comprising mostly of hair, rent, heating, and then food—mostly it's kale, tomatoes, eggplant, chicken giblets and health supplements. Too little exposure to sunlight here, her dark skin needs more.

And the tax deduction on her payslips—every single one of them—is robbery. She feels rage. And, for a moment, a deep and terrible sadness.

But the answer to her financial complications is right here.

She's looking at it.

The Setup

Hankering for money? That's all in the past.

Mayasa looks and looks at the ad. Being suspicious is a normal part of being a migrant. You don't land a safe foot into the unknown without hosting suspicion.

"Why are you here?"

"I need money," says Mayasa.

"I get you. You'll have it. But first, some questions. Any health conditions?"

"Joylessness."

"Allergies?"

"Fuckwits."

The dumb fool with a slow pen is asking questions from the back of a van that's a mobile office in an abandoned carpark at the outskirts of the city. Shipping containers litter the vacant lot.

"Do you like sex?"

"A lot, but I ditched a few bozos so I'm not getting any."

"Do you get orgasms?"

"You want to give me some?"

The girl's chewing and deadpan stare are annoying. "Something like that."

"A bit reverse," says Mayasa. "Normally I give it, but I'm not a hooker. Now let's stop fogging around and get to the point. Where's the money, and what must I do to get it?"

The girl points at the first container painted white.

"I had my suspicions at the company name: Tantralastic. If this is some dumb shit—"

"Next!" The girl blows a bubble, looks at the all-female queue.

The Supply

Mayasa has no clue why they want her to wear a transparent flow that resembles a kimono, and she's not sure she likes the arrangement after signing the forms. The container is partitioned, and there are grunts, groans, gasps and gurgles coming from cubicles.

But the sight of a woman, not a man, is reassuring, unless the charlatan is a madame who will usher potential clients. "Tea?"

"I like the African one. Rooibos. Three sugars. And milk."

"We don't have that one, but I can offer you piper mystica, vitalistas or elixir."

"What's in them?"

"Yam root, mushroom extract, lavender—"

"I'll take the yam root."

"Excellent choice. You need to relax."

"What I need is money."

"And you'll get it."

"But I don't want plugs, wands, bullets or lubes."

"There's none of that here. I need you to lie face down, legs splayed on this drum."

"Are you recording me in X-ray vision, and I'll find myself strewn on the dark web?"

"No."

"What are these cables?"

"I'll attach some to your head."

"Will it hurt?"

"No. Like this. See?"

"It's okay, I guess."

"Told you. Now the goggles. Here, you go—good. Finally, let's fit these bracelets. Perfect."

"What do you need me to do?"

"Use your deepest desire to catch the wave," the woman says, and dims the lights.

At first the illumination is lurid. Then Mayasa sees the radiant gold of a provocative African sun against the backdrop of a regal thorn tree. She feels the gentle wind of the savanna rustling grasslands in the wake of a cheetah's chase. She humps with the moon in its sacred beauty that summons a tidal wave. The sun, the wind, the moon... each in turn caresses the longing on Mayasa's tremulous lips, her perked up breasts, her opening thighs...

She wraps her legs around the drum.

"Oh. Ah. Right there. Yes!"

The Recycling

"Check your bank account," the woman says when Mayasa wakes. "We've transferred the money."

"Who cares about the money? Can I do the wave again?"

"Oh. You won't be having orgasms for a while."

"What?!"

"It's here—"

"In the fine print?"

"It's not forever—don't panic. Just a small side effect, you're not impaired. We harvest several years' worth of potential orgasms. Do you know how much energy a woman releases during her climax? You were a dynamo. And thank you."

"For what?"

"Think of your contribution to climate change. Participating in this revolutionary source of renewable energy that's naturally replenishable and sustainable to the planet. Not only that—it nourishes your deepest self. How do you feel now?"

"Wonderful!"

"Good. And when you miss that orgasm, think of the jeopardy in fossil fuels you've saved future generations."

"Is there a limit to technology?" Mayasa asks, even knowing it's rhetorical.

"Frankly, no."

"Why am I even afraid to ask?"

"It's fine. What's in the pipeline is nothing harmful. Tantralastic wants to be at the fore with competitive superiority to untap endless possibility. We're refining our technology and will soon start trials with male participants."

Mayasa raises her eyebrow. "The hell?"

The woman shrugs.

"Organic lotions, protein supplements, recycled water... Like I said. Endless possibilities."

Black Witch, Snow Leopard

The Rocking Valley

SAVANNAH stepped from a lone trail into an icy coldness that was untamed, but smelled ancient, sincere. It was a trail that refused to unlock any of its secrets through the valley.

The vale of black rocks connected the red hill and the tipping sea she was yet to understand—especially in her dreams. Nightmares were her undying dread. The dripping more than burning revealed nothing but the croak of the undead. An unseen exorcist manipulated her dreams, and they were filled with phantoms who stared as the sky looked down. Even when the ghosts and the sky weren't looking, her skin ached. She scratched it, and tweaked it, finally took to wearing snakeskin on her hands.

Now she trod on a fading grey whitewashed with memory from a place she'd been, yet never been. Its patterns were broken, staves worn away. There was no melody, just bloodshot feelings in a spectrum of abandoned light.

This earth under her feet was nothing but foreign. Not a monster like the sea, but still foreign. The image in her eye was of a trail of blood, then the splash of a woman who took the universe into her tears and bled salt that travelled and basked on lizards. Sometimes Savannah saw flames, hungry bonfires that gobbled feet, skin and bones.

She wanted to pluck petals, lay them on her eyes, take away the visions. But the valley was parched, and already she felt done like a roast.

Her mother died by drowning in the sea—this she knew, forgot how she knew, and disremembered if her mother was the tragic heroine of her dreams. She panicked at the thought she might recollect a woman of blue spit and no toes, eyes that changed colour between maps.

But time was lost, *tick, tick, shuffle, shuffle,* furtive as a jackal in something tragic that consumed. She slipped from black stone to black stone across the valley, *tick-tick shuffle-shuffle,* wishing she were a tree. Or the wind chasing traces of the leaves of a spreading baobab or sycamore uneven with afterimages of *tickytockleshuffle. Splash!*

The Devouring Grasslands

Qeow, my story vacillates between now and death. Qeowwww! It's a story of longing, haunting. Memory. Grrreeeeoowww! my mother said before her death. Greow, she said weakly, as two-legged monsters with a stick that spat fire took her skin, and then me.

The big water, qeow.

Save me. Qeeeeoowww!

"You, cutie devil," says Snatch, the two-legged with mud teeth.

Qeow, why are we hiding?

Greow. Because we're different. Sometimes being different, little one, makes us game.

Are we game like the big, fat African rat?

Especially game like the African rat—how easy to catch, so meaty to eat. Big ears that hear nothing. A long tail that drags on grassland, never loops on a tree branch. The foolish rat lives in a den but abandons shelter, even knowing it's soft-furred and slow moving. Fully game, greow to us. I'm glad you're not a picky eater.

Qeow, the rat is juicy.

Greow. A litter of rats, even juicier. Come, dear one. Time for your bath.

Purrrr, how are we different again, Mamm?

Purrrr. We have no rosettes to camouflage when we stalk creatures, climb trees, or prowl the savanna. The creatures we hunt see us. The pouched rat would see us if it cared to look, but it's too trusting in nature. Trusting and greedy. Eating, eating, always eating.

Why Mamm?

Why what, little one—why the rat's greedy?

Why don't we have colour? Rats are brown. Elephants are grey. Who took our colour, Mamm?

If you look closely, we DO have colour. Just white as snow.

What is snow?

It's full of light and feels like this.

Purrrr, like a licketty, lick?

Purrrr. Just colder, little one.

Qeow, can I see snow?

Greow. It's up on the mountain, right on the peak.

I want to find snow. Let's look for it in the dark. You said we see seven times better in the dark.

Yes, we are nocturnal. But it's too far to climb looking for snow. And we're too visible—the two-legged beast likes it there.

We didn't need the mountain for the two-legged beasts to find us. They came to the tall brown grass, flushed us out with banging and shouting.

Qeow, Mamm!

Greow. Hide, little one!

Mamm!

Grrreeeeoowww!

Mamm's shimmering blue eyes shone hate at a crowd of two-leggeds circling us and pointing sticks.

"Unbelievable!" one two-legged said. "It's a snow leopard and her cub."

Qeow, we're not snow leopards. Snow is far, far away, up on the mountains—

Grrreeeeoowww! Mamm said. Leave us!

A stick threw fire at Mamm.

Grrreeeeoowww! Hide, little one!

Mamm! No!

Grrreeeeoowww! I will tear and haunt you. I said leave us!

But the stick spat more fire, and Mamm—her graceful long body in mid-leap—crashed to the ground.

Qeow, Mamm! N-noo!

I nuzzled against her.

Mamm! Get up, run!

Little one, she said weakly. I told you to hide...

I purred against her chest and the beat of her heart. Ku-du. Ku-du.

Qeow, Mamm... I try to remember her different.

Not bleeding out on soil, but draped over a branch, a queen of the savanna. Mamm, she'd always warned me about the two-legged beasts.

I should have listened.

Perhaps if I'd not wandered away, leapt at the gold- and blood-winged butterfly... or the little bee-eater... or the red-billed oxpecker. If only I'd... qeow...

Hidden better...

The Healing Hills

The woman in a white flow looked back at Savannah—chained. Savannah howled, fought. She was stronger than two oxen, it took grown seamen to hold her.

"The snow will fall," the woman said, and stepped off the plank into the black sea.

Savannah woke startled and with much sweat from the nightmare's recurrence, the woman in white stepping, always stepping into the hungry sea.

Outside, the pitter-patter of a sleepy Sunday morning, grey and rainy.

She swept the hut she'd built with her hands, then scoured the highlands for medicinal herbs. Thistle, fennel, marjoram, chives, thyme... peppercorns, lilies of the valley. She lingered to her nostrils the saccharine scent of lavender—its bent to calm.

Normally she went through brush, wild hillside, picking out new flowers in winter's melancholy. Today, she carefully nurtured the lavender—it was what she needed to assuage a wound.

Demdike, the innkeeper's wife had managed to 'cut herself' again. Savannah knew exactly who did the cutting, and it wasn't the daughters: Chattox, the little minx with smoky quartz eyes, a colour in them that came and went. Whittle, the raven-haired woo that lads fell into puddles for. Redferne, the tall one and the stubbornness of her burgundy-haired head full of the shakes.

"It was definitely not them, your daughters. So tell me *who*?"

Demdike hung her head, silvered hair in a bun. She wouldn't look Savannah in the eye. "I ain' done nuffin' but fall, I swear."

"You and I both know falling had nothing to do with it. I've told you before, I'm saying it again. Put daylight between you and that soggy-head you wed."

"Ain' him, I swear. The bucket were there, right?"

"A hot bucket, then, was it? It cut and then burnt." Savannah reached to touch the burn, but Demdike snatched her tartan shawl over her wrist. "Aye. 'Twas an 'ot bucket."

Savannah handed her a jar. "Here—use this in a poultice for the... hot bucket." She touched Demdike gently on the shoulder. "I have two good ears, and some mulled wine."

"I better be off, wot, then."

"You're always welcome here, you know this."

"Hard Timmy'll be annoyed if 'e knew I came 'ere. They be lookin' fer me now."

"At least tell Redferne to collect her potion in the morrow. I'm nearly done making it."

"I don' know—"

"It will calm the shakes, Demdike."

"Aye," said the innkeeper's wife. She adjusted her mantle and hurried off holding her saffron skirt and the healing herbs down Red Hill, all the way to the Tilting Alehouse.

Savannah sighed and took back to the cluster of dark green leaves of mugwort in a pestle. She drummed the concoction, closed her eyes and swayed her head as she murmured invocation and sprinkled sage.

Her pounding talked a story until the sharp coolness gentler than mint, but with a bitter finish, overwhelmed the hut's smell of stick dolls and burning incense.

The Humping Sea

Qeow, I am sick, sick, sick. The vessel carrying us rocks, day and night it rocks, won't stop. But the two-leggeds down in the cargo hold are sicker. They are covered in sores and shit. Planks and chains everywhere. Bleak eyes like Mamm's when I crawled until I nuzzled and trembled against her dying body.

Ku-d... ku-d... her life fading until... silence, no heartbeat.

"Here, kitty." It's Snatch. He's tinkering with the door of my cage.

Qeow, what are you doing?

"Yer not one fer captivity."

He lifts me from the puddle upon which my cage stands, guarding the cargo hold.

Qeow, I hate water.

"I got somefin' to show yer," he says, as I tremble against him.

He throws me into a cabin infested with rats, burlap sacks and ghosts under a grey moon split half at the hoist of sunlight.

Qeow! I rush to get out, but he slams the door, locking me in.

Qeow, don't leave me.

"Make yerself useful," he says.

Don't leave me!

His footsteps fade away from the cabin.

At first, I mind the rats, so big, bigger, greedier and sharper-toothed than the fat, fat African rats. I ignore the bleeding rats, but they gnaw at me, goad me, until finally—

Qeeeeoowww!

So tasty.

"Good work," says Snatch. "Come here, little fella. Let's rub ya good."

Qeow.

The slayer of my mother. Should it matter whether he or a member of his crew did the killing?

Qeow.

"Good kitty. Hey—"

I leap off his lap and into the cargo hold.

"Greow," says a tightly-chained two-legged on the plank. "I so hungry, little leopard."

Qeow. I lick his sores, and the sores of the others, and strangely remember, and mourn, Mamm.

"I wish you could turn me, little leopard," the two-legged one groans.

Qeow, why are you in chains?

"They cut. Sore, itchy."

I find sacks of rotting maize, weeping yams, stained rice. I tear them, pull my head side by side to rip, as I saw Mamm do with tough meat. The ones in the cargo hold are grateful as I feed them the way Mamm pushed meat into my mouth.

But Snatch finds me.

We sail, and sail. We pass a ship graveyard that's not as bad as the absence of an elephant graveyard weighed with tusks, shadows and winter bones. A wretched hopelessness in the spectrum of a calf's corpse in white bones shined oily in a vultures' feast. I listen to the wind, to the faint but familiar beat of my dead mother's heart in it. Calling, calling me.

Kudu. Kudu.

I feel a deep and terrible sadness. Mamm, are you there?

Echoes of our synchronised heartbeats. *Kudu kudu kududu.*

Qeow, are you?

Her scent of protection and wilderness speaks to me. Her sweet, sweet scent of something safe that isn't a lie. Inside my freeze I bask in the winter sun of her heartbeat. Thumping in bittersweet, gleaming with healing, memory and promise. She's here, she's there, she's waiting. Not yet. Her shimmering blue eyes stream light to my core.

Kukudududu.

I cuddle against the silence of her ancient heartbeat. *Kudu. Kudu.*

The sailing, the fat rats and the cargo hold teach me to replace the smog of melancholy with the earnest of doing. Foghorns blow across the horizon between land and sea. We come to a place called Cape of Good Hope, and I hear Snatch say something about the Brower Route, and going to the Dutch East Indies, then all the way to a place called England.

Snatch puts me to his chest. "Yer fetch a pound or two. It'll keep tha young'uns feedin'. Yer know about hunger?"

Qeow.

He rubs my chin.

Purrrr. Please don't judge me. I am alone, empty. I need to feel, and Snatch is a connection to my past, until I see—

Land! Qeow!

"But, kitty! That ain' England!"

Qeow! I nearly fall off the ship in my excitement. Then I remember Mamm without her white royal skin. Mamm dripping crimson on savanna grasslands.

I leap into the cold, black waters and paddle for land. Now I know how Mamm caught fish and crabs.

"Kitty! What 'appen to trust? I thought we had somefin'."

Qeow. I don't trust anyone who's slayed Mamm, I yell back. I don't know how I do it, but I glide across the water as if it's the most natural place to be.

"He can go!" cries Snatch, and I wonder if it's an exclamation of release, or at my speed.

I turn, uncertain if I'm goading, gloating or protecting my pride.

Qeow, I don't know about you but, actually, I'm a she.

I wash into land and run, run, run!

Grrreeeeoowww! Hide, little one! says Mamm in the wind.

Run, run, rundily run. All things run-run rundily run. The tongueless birds rearrange their wings. Clap their beaks on cold-cold bark. Run run rundily run. This is not my home. Like. Ever. Shadowed nests so dull in fog. I close my eyes to catch some light. This place so dark, so cold, oh brrrr. Run run rundily run. I want my frii-eends. Where you my frii-eends? The sun sunny bird jacko jacana. Locki locust bird-bird birdy. Pulse-pulse. I want my frii-eends. Where you my frii-eends? Oh crany crane-crane weave-weave-weave weaver. Oxy-pecker bee bee-eater. Pulse. Pulse. Br-br so co-old. This place so c-old! I want my mamm! Are you my mamm? Why am I hiding? Because I'm different. And different makes me game. Run, run, rundily run. Runrunrundilyrunrunrun.

Qeow, I've been running, day and night. I feel like I'm moving in the wrong direction. The birds here are scrawny, nothing like the juicy ones of the savanna grasslands. But they too are crafty—I can't catch them. I dream of the white-faced fish eagle, always paired. The yellow weaver birds, always vigilant, how territorial. The grey-crowned crane, sometimes dancing, jumping, bowing with a booming call. The red-billed oxpecker, chattering in a flock, each bird diligent plucking hair from the wildebeest. I'd give a paw for a mere glimpse of the annoying feathered locust bird!

One afternoon I see a two-legged little one hoisting skewered rats, still bleeding, on his shoulder. So hungry. They're thinner than the fat African rat, but, oh, so shareable.

Qeow, I like rats. Are you lost like me?

He's no-skinned, ghost-eyed and the eyes grow bigger. He drops his load and yells, "Daaaad!" A big two-legged comes running with a stick that spits fire. He'll take my skin!

Runrunrundilyrunrunrun.

Qeow, so hungry. What's this? More two-leggeds! Too many of them! What place is this?

Grrreeeeooowww! Hide, little one! says Mamm in the wind.

"Grab yerself a bargain!" someone is yowling. Near him, two-legged beings who look like the ones from the cargo hold—thin and weak and in chains—are lined up on a platform on the other end. On the far side, more chained ones eat something mushy from a trough.

I watch in stealth behind a barrel of something smelly and sticky like the fresh dung of a baby kudu. And then I see it, out yonder, something white and splayed. My mother's skin—cut from her body as she breathed her last.

I heave and throw up the tiny fish still in my stomach.

The Unyielding Market

The call of a beating heart astonished Savannah. *Kudu kudu kududu.* She woke up to an urge, a deep desire, for satin and silk. She couldn't understand it, but the urge besieged her feet and she found herself walking to the market.

She ran her hand through cotton, silk, satin, even pelts in a few stalls. "Is this unicorn?" she asked, at the price of fox.

The owner laughed. "But I 'ave wildcat, deer, red squirrel. And look—these are feathers of a golden eagle—"

Kudu kudu kududu. Savannah moved towards the faint beat, and found a stall that sold corn, fish and hides. On the far side were the livestock: goats, piglets, rabbits, duck, bobwhite quail, calves, ruffed grouse... She listened for the heartbeat—it wasn't here. She took one last look at the pheasant, bought a fowl, then at the craft stalls with their necklaces, anklets, rings and pendants.

She was turning away when, again, she heard it. She followed its drumming... *kudu*... *kudu*... and saw the man inspecting slaves. He was a furious little man running impatient fingers over a naked girl's teeth. He arranged his plaid kilt as if hiding something, and groped the girl's breasts for firmness, then took a whip from the kilt's belt and raised a hand to test her mettle.

Savannah's eyes rolled, her arms spread, and a chant fell from her mouth. The man collapsed to the ground as if himself struck. He rose, all shaky, abandoned his flogger on the ground—never put it back into the belt of his plaid kilt, and scrammed, bare-legged from the market.

Savannah followed him with her eyes until he was gone. She didn't understand it, the chant. What she understood was that it worked to save the girl, albeit for a moment. She wondered if she could—

She lifted the flogger, looked around, dropped it. Too many merchants to flog away, and they'd notice if she tried to free the slaves. And what was that over there?

It stood at the far elbow of the market—a black statue of a boxer on a pyre. Savannah moved closer to study it. She peered at the plaque, and pulled back from it. She felt sick. It wasn't a boxer on a pyre. It was the torched corpse of a runaway slave, burnt alive.

She stepped away, aghast, and fell into a baby leopard.

The Whispering Hut

Qeow, just because I listen to the heartbeat in the wind doesn't mean I have to believe in it. But I do. When it told me to run, I ran for three days, three nights straight. When it told me to hide, I hid. That's how I found myself behind a barrel in a market selling flesh swarming with famine and bondage. On each face—some eating mush from a trough—I saw a memory that wasn't a happy ending. It was a memory that was a haunting, an Absolute Everything, without which its bearer would go mad.

The wind says, who taught you this game?

I learned from the time I was born.

But I don't say this. Instead, I say, qeown't you the wind?

My heart is an untidy garden, dark clouds eddying patches of it. The rest is grizzled with trees. I look at the black witch whose face is a sundial, shadows in her eyes. I need the axis of her promise, any promise, but her leafless stare puts the words right out of me.

Would she... might she...?

Her hands grab me. "What have we here?" Her voice rolls and rolls in grassland gust. She looks at the vomit, then at the leaking barrel. "I see why you smell of fish and ale," she says.

The bald two-legged witch takes me in her arms up a red hill to a hut. I'm too astonished, perhaps too tired or petrified to protest.

She peers at me. I peer at her from underneath the straw bed.

"Oh, what big eyes you have. The colour of the sky."

Qeow.

"Here, little leopard, is where you say: *The better to see you.*"

Qeow.

"My word, so frightened, so curious. What are you expecting to see?"

Qeow.

"No one will jump you."

Qeow.

"I like your enthusiasm."

Qeow.

"But do you like food?"

Purrrr.

She reaches with a bowl, and I crawl backwards towards the wall.

"Trying to get a bit of darkness?"

Qeow.

She tries to flush me with a broom, and I shuffle into another corner.

"Will you just barrel from one hiding place to another?"

Qeow.

"You're pretty special, little leopard."

Qeow.

"Okay, I'm not looking. Try this. Here, yummy."

Purrrr.

It's a bowl of arrow roots soaked in goat milk. I gobble the lot.

"Good. I see you're not picky."

Purrrr.

"Pale blue eyes, mmhhh. You're an albino leopard, aren't you? Question is—how did you get here?"

Qeow.

"My name's Savannah. What shall we call you?"

Qeow, they hurt my mamm.

"Let's call you Snow."

Qeow, no.

She inches forwards on elbows and knees.

"What's that, you say?"

Qeow, I'm not a snow leopard. Snow is up on the mountains, far, far away.

"Fine. Your name's Kiaow." She strokes my nose.

Qeow.

"What's this? You like this scratching. Right here under the chin, Kiaow?"

Purrrr.

"Well, Kiaow. Welcome to the gloaming."

Purrrr.

"You're so secretive. Won't kill you if I see you poop!"

Qeow.

"So elusive, all the time on your own. Under the straw bed is not rapture."

Qeow.

"How solitary. I am your *friend*. Friends don't hurt you."

Qeow, they do. His name is Snatch.

I crawl further back under the straw bed.

Savannah waits me out until I sleep. In my dream is a dead gazelle, fat maggots wriggling on its skin. Falling out of its mouth, squeezing out of closed eyes.

Qeeeeoowww!

I throw up on the gloaming.

"Is this deliberate?"

Qeow.

"A bit of a mess, little leopard. Let's work this down. See this? It's sage."

Qeow.

"You won't like it—it's a bitter finish."

Qeow.

"And this is lavender." She grips me by the neck.

"Together, they will sort your vomiting."

Qeeeeoowww!

"Don't fight it."

Qeeeeoowww!

"Don't pee on me! And don't scratch."

Qeow.

"Sleep on it..."

"Qe-o-w."

"Hey," she pokes me in the ribs. "Are you awake? Look what I got. Yum-yummy."

Purrrr.

"If I didn't know better... Is this a turn?"

Purrrr.

"Here, under the neck like this?"

Purrrr.

"This is magic. Our stars are together. Whose will wane first?"

Purrrr.

"You definitely need a wash."

Qeeeeoowww!

"Stop fighting. And no nipping at me either! The water's not that cold."
Can't you licketty-lick like Mamm?

"Following me, are we? Come closer, I don't bite."

Qeow.

"Fine, be like that. This here—" she shows me a flower, "is of the daisy family. It can grow up to six foot high. Yes, taller than you."

Qeow.

"These yellow-reddish ones are fine as a tonic—they cure colic. But these dark-green ones are the best for cramps and constipation. Have you pooped lately?"

Qeeeeoowww!

"Don't be indignant, I won't make you eat them. See here—these silvery white hairs underneath the leaves. They treat worms. Come now. I said I don't bite."

Suddenly, there's a knock on the door. A fresh-faced female two-legged with raven hair falls into the hut.

"Miss Savannah. Miss!"

"What's wrong, Whittle? That fool of a man—is it your mother?"

"It's Redferne. The shakes are killing her in the kitchen."

The Tilting Alehouse

Savannah raced to the alehouse, awash with gossip of gallows and ten people hanging in a row at the castle. She brushed aside the murmurings, swept into the kitchen where Redferne was convulsing on the floor between pots and pans. Her head lolled, her eyes rolled back.

The innkeeper's wife was trying to push a wooden spoon between the girl's teeth.

"Stop," said Savannah. "I said stop!"

The kitchen-help crowd parted.

"A wooden spoon will only do harm."

Savannah turned Redferne gently onto her side. She loosened her belt. The girl was wearing a short woollen, close-fitting coat. Savannah loosened it too.

"Give me that shawl."

Savannah made a pillow of it, rested the girl's head on it.

"Now off!" she clapped her hands. "Everyone off! Get out. Get out!"

The crowd cleared. Redferne stared into space.

"Hey, darlin'," her mother said.

"Feel better, sweetie?" Savannah said. "You'll be all right. I'm here to make sure. There, there, lovie." She stroked her cheek with the back of her fingers.

She looked at Demdike. "Your daughter didn't come for the potion as I asked."

"'Er father forbade it."

"I see." Savannah's voice was stern, but kindly when she turned back towards Redferne. "Here, here. Better already, no? Let's have some lavender tea. It will calm you."

It was darkened by now. Exhausted, Savannah sat alone at the dim-lit bar of the alehouse, aware she was the only woman ordering. All the rest were serving. It was not long after midday, but the Tilting Alehouse was packed. She studied the brickwork, and its announcements near the stairways to the vaulted cellar for rooms to rent, lodgers welcome, as if it were a matter of the utmost importance. She knew too well there'd be no lodgers in the cellar. That was for fortified wine and vintage ale straight from a brew-house.

"More, luv?" asked the waitress.

"Another wine. Small."

"On its way, guv. Will ya be havin' a bite?"

"What's on special?"

"Everyfing's on special."

"Oh, yes?"

The innkeeper in his apron and hat of hair glared at her from the other end of the counter. Despite Savannah helping to heal his daughter, he refused to near her as if she were a leper.

"Scotched veal, pottage," the waitress was saying. "Potted pork, fruit tart, rice pudding, sheep's cheese, blueberry pie, bread. Wut will yer 'ave guv?"

Horses neighed in the stables.

Savannah noticed a tall man and what might have been his wife staring intently across the packed alehouse in her direction. He wore a long coat, waistcoat and breeches. Clean crop, severe eyes.

"That's Hono'rable Smoko fer yer. Justice of Peace from London."

"Is that right," said Savannah.

"They got all the fashion in London, right guv?" the waitress said.

"That, they do." Savannah studied the wife's long-waisted bodice, her silken overskirt draped and pinned up behind.

"Ain' they perfect?"

"That they aren't. Especially this one making his way—too much devilment in his eyes."

The Justice of Peace was parting folk with his presence, as he approached.

"I hear you've been causing headaches," he said.

"I find some confidence in that," said Savannah.

"Confidence is a dangerous prospect in this world."

"And why is that?"

"For one who creates chaos, you're one to ask."

"She's a sickness eater!" a voice piped from the back.

"Brings trouble wiv the cows!" another shouted. "Me cows been sick since this un showed." He was slapping his hands, throwing his arms.

"I'd say maybe you're sick," threw back Savannah evenly. "Come and see me about what's ailing you. We might just cure you."

Men guffawed—the laughter was crude in a way that implied a different curing.

"Watch it," said the Justice of Peace. "Such accusations against you, might catch fire."

"Yeah, wotchit, right," someone echoed. "Yer might cotch fire, witch."

"They call me Smoko," said the Justice of Peace. "Commissioned by the Crown to maintain public order. I smoke 'em out. Witches.'

"I'm sure you do," said Savannah. "In black robes and a wig."

"The wig might be handy for one thing first." His look was knowing. "That hush shop you run."

"I'm not selling anything in my hut."

"Them branches an' leaves on the door tell differen'!" someone yelled.

"Tut-tut. Stealing from the Crown—*severely* punishable," said the Justice of Peace.

"I do nothing of the sort."

"The last ones I punished found themselves hooded in rows of ten at the gallows."

"If you'll excuse me—"

"By all means. I'm sure we'll meet again."

"I doubt that very much." Savannah looked at the waitress. "I believe I've just lost my appetite." She palmed the waitress a coin, and turned to leave.

But the crowd was pushing towards her with a growing cry. "Light 'er up!" The chant started in a corner, spread like flames across the alehouse. "Light 'er up!"

"Let's see you glide through that mob baying blood," said the Justice of Peace.

"Light 'er up!"

Qeeeeoowww!

Everyone turned towards the sound, with a mixture of emotion at the sight of a baby leopard white as snow.

"Ain' it cute?"

Qeeeeoowww! said Kiaow, poised to leap at the Justice of Peace.

"I've got a thumping boot," he said. "Don't let that kitty near me."

"I won't take any more of your time," agreed Savannah. She whistled, and Kiaow's momentum carried the cub forward into her arms.

Purrrr.

"I'm happy to see you too." She rubbed his chin. "Good to see you get involved, but some filth's not worth fighting."

Purrrr.

"You're a keeper, you know."

That night the cub lay on Savannah's bed, its paw on her chest. She believed intensely in the power of tragedy. How it made her forget. But now she remembered. Love made her remember.

Together, they listened to the wind, to the faint but familiar beats of dead mothers' hearts calling, calling.

Kudu. Kudu.

Kudu kudu kududu. Kudu. Kudu.

The leopard cub snored.

Suddenly, a roar, and the hut collapsed. A mob with pitchforks and torches dragged Savannah and the cub out into the night.

The Judging Castle

"Wot cow got no 'air on the 'ead?"

"'Ave a look at 'er nose!"

"Aye! It's a witch nose."

"Big as a pancake." The pack roared with glee.

"Not a pancake. 'Tis a crumpet!" Ribald laughter. "Honest guv!"

"It's a cookie, right?"

Kiaow refused to leave Savannah's side as the villagers piled insults and accusations.

"Bet she wiv no toes—'ave a look at them boots!"

"Aye. No fingernails eiver—why is she wearin' snake gloves?"

"She ain' no witch!" cried Demdike's daughter Chattox. "'Er eyes don' change colour."

"Tell 'er ter spit—I swear it's blue."

"Aye. No bloke knows where she come from!"

"Out of the Valley of Black Rocks. Would I lie ter you? She's a witch, right!"

"Flog 'er!"

"Drown 'er!"

"String 'er!"

"Light 'er up honest!"

Qeeeeoowww!

They pushed her along a dark trail down the hill, the crowd roaring. Someone played a flute, as if it were a feast day.

They arrived at the great, big castle where they held trials. And there he was, the Justice of Peace.

"I said we'll meet again."

"And here we are."
"Flog 'er!"
"String 'er!"
"Light 'er up!"
"Drown 'er!"

Savannah remembered her mother on the slave ship. Hands tied behind her back, composed on a plank. *You will never enslave me*, she said, and that was her crime. Punishable by death. *You can take my body, everything a mess. But that's all you get.*

Savannah relived an escape, and the water's pull. How she gave a shout that she thought was a call, a last call, but then something happened. A soft touch closed her eyes, and she was slipping, slipping. She woke sodden, sandwashed on a seashore. A voice that was a nonvoice in her head said, *It's okay.*

Out yonder beyond the black sea she saw a valley and a highland.

She leapt to bare feet, started running for the valley.

"She didn' do nuffin', I swear!" Savannah looked at Demdike, who'd uttered these words.

The crowd was livid. "Ere's anuvver witch. 'Ave a look at 'er daughters. That un—colour in 'er eyes that comes and goes, right? That un—'aunted by ravens. That un—she's a red devil, right!"

"There ain' anyfink wrong wiv wot is mine," bellowed the innkeeper. "Keep yer problems wiv this one. You 'eard she sellin' 'ush wine. Payin' no taxes like normal good folk. Embezzlin' the Crown. And aye, she eats malady. I don't know wot she's done ter Redferne. But the gal is livin' proof."

"Flog 'er!"
"Drown 'er!"
"String 'er!"
"Light 'er up!"

"No one's doing any flogging or drowning or stringing. Or lighting," said the Justice of Peace. "Until I say so."

The cawing crowd repeated her crimes, and all the grudges anyone ever had.

"Only witches 'ave large nose holes."

"Since she come 'ere, me cows been sick!"

"And wot 'appened ter the rain, isit? It don' fall right."

"Me spuds come out blue."

"Light 'er up honest!"

The gavel fell.

Demdike pushed through the crowd, palmed Savannah a tiny pouch.

"I'm bloody well grateful fer wot yer done fer me and me daughters. I swear, the good Lor' shame me. This is the best I can do fer yer. Burnin ain' no pleasant, I swear. If yer like, I can pay fer the executioner ta strangle yer first."

"Demdike. You've done more than enough. Now spend your focus on yourself, and your daughters. I can take care of myself."

Awaiting her fate at dawn, she woke, the night a serpent. Twisted dusk, quelled dreams in which she wasn't a victim. But every so often in those visions she couldn't utter a thing, as a swarm of black locusts buzzed between her teeth.

Hers was a language of blood and water, untellable secrets from pamphlets or palimpsests of gone lives speaking her name in parody and discomfort, fading, fading... to visions of snow or rain across eons.

The Roaring Pyre

The night is lost. Past the estuary, my past life pushes toes into wet sand. A cocoa-skinned baby falls into the water, picking palmfuls of sand, unfrightened of jellyfish gliding along arms. There's a bridge of wood and rope above stones and a simmering surface. The sun's rays are like the eyes of a beast twinkling back and forth on the breathing tide, formless in death without a body already snatched.

I rouse with a start.

Savannah's in trouble. By the shiver of daybreak, she'll be gone. Bound to a stake.

Qeeeeoowww!

The crowd laughed. "Best yer can do, pussy cat?"

Qeeeeoowww!

Time was lost, tick, tick, shuffle, shuffle, in something tragic that consumed. Savannah wished she were the wind across the valley, tick-tick shuffle-shuffle, tickytockleshuffle. She remembered a woman of blue spit and no toes, eyes that changed colour between maps. Her mother was her true heroine.

She looked at the leopard cub crying in lonesomeness at the base, refusing to abandon her even in those last moments.

The moon is broken, or perhaps it's my heart. There she is, my Savannah, at the stake.

Qeow! Don't leave me.

She gazes into my soul. "You've excited the crowd. Go home now, Kiaow."

Qeow!

"You're loved," she says calmly. "And that's enough."

I pull fangs and claws, and stare down the crowd.

"Kiaow! What are you doing?"

Qeow, I've found my new mamm.

"Might as well burn 'er wiv 'er pet familiar."

"Aye!"

"Kiaow, little one, I told you to go home!"

"Grab that kitty!"

"Kiiaoww! Hide, little one! Run!"

Qeeeeoowww! Leave us alone!

"That the best yer can do, kitty?"

Savannah's eyes are closed, her lips moving in a chant.

Someone throws a flaming torch at the foot of the pyre, and the straw catches.

Just then, there's a terrible howl from the skies and a white wind full of ice swirls from it. It's a coldness like no other. It's a whiteness full of light and a coldness that is—

Snow.

The skies opened and a woman in a white flow, cloaked in frost, stepped from the heavens.

"The snow will fall," she said, and stepped off the snowy plank into the flames.

A snowstorm sweeps across the panic-stricken crowd. Above their cries, I heard my mother's beating heart. *Kudu. Kudu.*

Grrreeeeoowww! The crowd burst into new cries at my sound.

GRRREEEEOOWWW!

I leap and lope and soar above heads and the dying flames choking in snow. The momentum topples the stake and Savannah and I crash to the ground.

"My word!"

Savannah was unsure what moved her more: Kiaow's new roar, or the ghost of her own mother cascading downwards in snow.

Kiaow gnaw-cut the ropes that bound Savannah to the fallen stake.

Purrrr, so this is snow.

"What's this—licketty lick? If I didn't know better... I'd say you're fond of me."

Purrrr.

"We're kindred, hey? Now let's find someplace we belong."

The Unending Tale

And that is the legend of the black witch and the snow leopard who vacillate between now and death, no waning. Just a shine of together stars talking in story and a murmuration of daughters and mothers full of longing, full of haunting.

Memory.

Kudu. Kudu. Kukudu. Kudu.

Neuter

The Hunt

NEUTER IS DRAWN to a shimmer of mirrors, accented illumination from a disco ball flashing multi-hues on a DJ misjudging his skill, bodies 'shaking-it' on the dance floor. She sheds her skin, travels down onto a walkway bathed in moonlight. Streetlamps are in a dazzle, bouncing back her glow of eyes, her hair.

She takes measures to impose. Faces of drunks, yahoos and the misplaced shadow her dusk stroll. Swish, sashay. She butters their hunger as it melts toward her. Perhaps it's an aura about her that franks their conviction she's what they desire—but how to approach her, in which version, on what move? Their yearning is a desert, a desolate calling at the edge of something that's always a bigger story. But, too soon, she'll swoon to the skies abandoning humanity, her eerie glow to the heavens or the hells pulling away from them.

She allows a stamp on her wrist from a ripple-muscled bouncer. Tolerates fishbowl cocktails that glow in the dark. She'll listen to conversations, overlook spilt booze, wafts of smoke on leather jackets, an air of cheap sex on the dance floor, and graffiti on the toilet walls. Jostling potentials eager to catch her interest will pay extra for the VIP zone with lounge chairs and a rope.

She's poisonous and they know it for they can sense it—she sees it in their approach. They fall silent through the barrier, but a compulsion to speak to her overwhelms them. Fear touches their adulation as they tell her of their dreams.

"I die for you," a clean face says with a hint of slur. "Every night."

She likes his eyes, moonstone, but—unlike the gemstone and the soothing it offers—it's he who craves assurance, and she not offering it. "You're a screamer. Get me a drink."

"What kind—"

"Be deadly. Astonish me." She flicks him off with a nail on the cheek as if it has a fly on it, or he's one.

Her response is an art, a spectre that gobbles love chants, venom that turns humanity into leaves, crisp and hissing in a whisper of scales that brings them back to the nightclub again, and again.

They dream of escape, as colour edges the neon lights of some other dusk spot where she peeled some fool off the heel of her boot. There, yet again, the finesse of luminol transformed into prism misread the vibe of night caves and self-destruction where, just before dawn, men and women scrapped for her attention. She stood still as a silhouette refracted in the moon's gaze giving way to luscious crimson in clips the world never s a w.

The Observer

Neuter's a big gal, owns the space. And the dreads—as in locks. She owns them, too. She's wearing good-looking dimples that don't flash often, 'cept when she abandons a b r e a k i n g heart knowing it'll st ay H O P E F U L.

I've seen her kind, often. They make the journey in inspired moves, plunging at full moon from the skies. They fly in, devoid of colour from the sides—you see them right there, at the corner of your eye. You wonder if you imagined the flicker, as they trickle in smart and play risk, creating indecision in pockets of Earth where the forest chatters, the wind chimes, the night hums and thunder clatters.

You know those invaders who dance your dreams? Slumber you in propositions filled with baby shadows? They're real. Transgressions who night-walk across your wilderness. They are at ease with a moon that paints her face with wine and spice, that leaves footprints on souls.

Neuter smiles at me. Her lightning hair—it's a sizzle, white, tinged with the colours of the rainbow—reminds somewhat of doom. She doesn't care to be invisible. She smells of lilies and carnations. Overwhelming, yet memory. She smells of citrus and freshly mown grass. Custard, bitter orange and spice.

She twirls the amber liquid in her flute. I've put her in the VIP of the VIP—bouncers cordoning her from the fresh-faced throng swelling into a riot.

"Smother," she says. "Fools."

"I give you that." I nod at a strapping kid Big Moose has by the scruff of the neck. The kid has good cheekbones, a close crop around his fringe. Generally, the no-trouble kind but now he's frothing. Big Moose splits the crowd, holds insurrection with the unlucky chap destined for face down on a curb. Bodies in the throng throw themselves to close the gap Big Moose left, but the other bouncers know their act.

"Don't you reckon that kid's still a teenager?"

Neuter holds my gaze, intimate for a moment. She breaks into a smile. "Drats, Jim-O, you're right. Opportunity gone begging."

"I'm thinking this whole shit's getting over your head."

She laughs, the closing peal of a tiny bell. "You're a ripper, Jim-O. Talking nonsense—who do you think you are?"

"You said it, not a screamer. You won't see me flickering back and forth, looking for identity from the gaze of a woman, like those randos over there."

"On the blocks as always, never holding back."

"Unlike the poor souls you crisp." I study how her finger caresses the wine glass. "Or shall I say, unlike *you*? Holding back, I mean."

Again, her laughter. "No, no, no."

"Yes, yes. Something keeps you coming back. Yet you give so little of you."

"Perhaps what I want is right here. A leaf cannot focus when it's dead. But I can. All at once. Watch you intently. That's giving much of myself, mmhh?"

"That so?" I pull a fresh batch of flutes from the dishwasher beneath the counter, arrange them on the overhead rack. "I never thought of you as dead. But you do watch me, I give you that."

"I see your thoughts, Jim-O. How you struggle with the abstract of your entireness."

"I'm not struggling with anything. And what the fog's *an entireness*?"

"Oh, yes, you are fraught. And your sense of self is a question from something borrowed that vanishes as it forms. Your craving will never settle until you summon the right question to push you out of the jungle and into a gushing river pregnant with nothing sinister."

I smile. "I don't need a river."

"No, you don't."

"And I don't need a shrink."

"What you need are stones in a riverbed," she says.

"Let me assess my own options."

"As I said, you crave something. Perhaps a closer look, a burst of spring. Right there—that's your riddle."

"Is it?"

"You tell me." She rubs her neck in a sensual way.

"You ask a lot of questions. So now I'm your riddle. Must truly bug you that I don't jump at your beckon like those fools you woo."

Her laughter again. "Tell me about your mother."

"Fuck's wrong with you?"

"I'm always the demon."

But later, once I've locked up and climbed to the loft, I ponder Neuter's goading. Why she should bring my mother into the equation is not quite beyond me, because Neuter is a stirrer. She reads people, and knows my detachment is self-preservation.

What a mother tells you is the eclipse of what you're made. Her scent is the vanilla spice, a summer sweetness that casts sun through the winter of your shell. Her memory is the black beauty elderberry that brings you moondust and stardust, the stuff of which you're made, who you think you are. I don't have a mother. Buddy murdered her, never paid for it. So I don't have a father either. He can breathe across the line all the wants. Why does he call? Why now? He invades, a phantom faded with age. Time has run him down to chaff.

What I have is Aunt April. Soaked in chocolate mud, sprayed with wattle seed. That's the warm smell of home in her house where she raised me. Aunt April, earthy as a beet. She's aniseed and myrtle. Bush honey. Her love is caramelised to last. She can be pungent, hot tempered. Her words are fermented, spicy, a fresh perspective, especially when offered with iced hibiscus tea—fruity, sweet and sour all at once. A lot of sour lately. Her multi-dimensional complexity finds unease with my dating habits.

"Your father went down that very path. See how he turned out."

The Clues

Grief is a pedal to the medley accompanying instructions to a novel that's so not in vogue. Tastes are a fad and have moved on to assemble diagrams and translations for a documentary on suffering into the future. Grief distils lonesomeness and unfakeable commitment, any promise of claim. Tomorrow is looking cold and wet, and a shaking-down is not a dressing-up.

Jim-O gobbles and spits women. Even as he does, April wonders if he sweats and trembles wondering if there are question marks inside his drowning. Grief takes its time to an iridescent dawn beyond the surface. Doors behind doors in crisscross with silent weeping. Whimpers straight from a nursery awash with the bric-a-brac of lost parents, whose imprint is unclear at best of times to everyone. Years of struggle in retrospect add doors-to-doors-to-doors. Even with boots and umbrellas, how does one escape, let alone get.

Anywhere?

It's not easy for a man who lost his mother as a boy. Buddy could tell him that, but Jim-O won't listen. And Buddy is no less broken.

The Hunt

It's a new dusk, more fools stampeding over Neuter. But she prefers the bar, Jim-O.

"I don't do people," he says.

"Is that why you're immune to me? What if I'm not 'people'?"

"I don't know what you want from me, Neuter."

She downs a shot. "More of that brilliance, if you please."

He tops her. "That's a slippery nipple."

"I'm not sure I'm the person you want to be telling that. And you wonder what I want from you. What if all I want is a swoon?"

"Isn't that boring? Everyone fawning—can't I stand out?"

"Your problem, Jim-O, is online. When you spend this long on dating apps, you're bound to lose something."

"My soul?"

"And it haunts the space between the keyboard and the chair. You delete a connection with a keystroke, take small steps, big steps, meet another, then another. But you can never forge more than a flitting sense of wonderment tinted in pixel, commemorated in a profile swaddled in plagiarism."

"Your language is Babel. I don't know what you're talking about, Neuter."

"You search for ribcages—your very Eve. But online will give you nothing. No Eve will ever fit your damaged self."

"Stay safe. There's a killer out there."

Neuter l a u g h s.

The Observer

Each new profile is a backup to a new world that opens with fat promises, but imprints its wrinkled self in endless repetitions that decay your very c o r e. Sw ipe. Ag ain S W I P E!

Luscious39681hashtag is a flirty one.

How's your imperfect self? she says.

Tall, lit. Amazing. Are you an intern? I say.

Nah, just my brother's keeper.

Welcome to the boneyard. You wanna tip?

Amazing.

No ribcage here—unless you have a warrant, or a DNA match.

Is that so?

Yeah. Are you really your brother's keeper?

Well, it's not you. Your name's not William.

No regrets.

Yep, trust that—your tiny, bruised self. So gnarly. Who stole your wife?

Well, I—

Ah, wait, you did it to yourself.

Nup. Lost her in an embarrassment of riches. Or let's just say: a richness of embarrassments. That's right.

Sometimes that works, and I get laid. As in sex-texting.

Neuter asks, "What's sex texting?"

"You're a mind reader now? I'm not telling you shit."

Her laughter, that closing chime of a baby bell. She hugs her shoulders in a soft pink gown. It's a clinger with a neck choker, a bare back.

"You find me hilarious?"

"Look who's over their head," she purrs.

"Be careful, I might say you like me."

She leans into me. "I like what you host," she says. "A deep and terrible sadness."

"You know I'm at sea with this emotions thingy you're doing."

"Don't be."

"Not used to talking feelings. Let's not start now."

"I can crank them up," she offers.

"Go home, Winter Melon."

The Clues

If you stare long enough at silvered nightlights thirsty for noticing, what's wild yet delicate is cradled in curled or straight lonesomeness that's no paradigm shift as it's always been there. The next step is that you bring together what's left and quantify its expected lifespan into bleeding-edge frames that make sense of small creatures in dissolving bones. And, even as you look, you are no less centred, receding or packed away in dashes of abstraction.

Aunt April feels it's time. Jim-O needs the truth.

The Hunter

One dancer's head is bowed, his hands all stiff. Another's rolling his hips. "Look, look!" says Jim-O. "Why don't you take the dance floor?"

Neuter shakes her head. "Too fancy on the footwork. His kind are redundant, but they demand with interest."

When you know to read the vibe, you get what she means. Neuter's a picker—she draws first blood. Even as she tweaks and polishes wounded hearts.

"You can handle that—interest?" Jim-O's leaning with a dishcloth across the counter.

She takes his hand. "I know you think I'm a player. Well, I'm happy with that—others have said worse. But I'm just catching up on living. Things I should have done before..." Her voice is an oboe. Her new laughter is forced. "I'm just living, is all. And it's about individual brilliance, long and high. An unreachable bar."

"You're on the wings, always on the wings. That's unreachable."

"I'm never selfless to a fault," she says, caressing his arm. "Such beautiful hands."

"The better to tear you?"

They laugh together.

They are buzzed on moonlight. Tonight, he's briefly immortal. She's eternally immortal. His eyes dance with grave music, the kind that sprouts from a hymnbook inside the chapel of a small village and florets in greyscale mermaids on rocks into a cathedral.

His smart phone r i n g s.

The Observer

Another private number. I won't steer his no n-C O N V E R S A T I O N.

"You can breathe all you like at the end of the phone. I know it's you. Buddy—get a grip."

Silence.

"You weren't there for me, growing up, mate. I don't know why it's fine by you to give a fog now."

More breathing.

"Fuck this. Being a dad is more than a gamete. I bled black and white because crimson was too costly. Times have changed from when I needed you first class. Now you're return-to-sender. No postmark required. Keep calling, and I'll get a restraining order."

Neuter knuckles the counter. Her lightning hair sparkles. "That's a bit rough."

"Me? Never."

"Then why are your eyes sabres?"

Suddenly, I'm game to the avalanche that is Neuter. A catastrophe that smells of candles and clouds. Citrus and freshly-mown grass. A scent that overwhelms yet brings memory.

I take her hand. "I can lock up. Show you my pad."

She pulls her hand, as if my touch burns.

"No. No!"

The Clues

"It's past midnight! And you've had a few. You almost never drink on the job!"

"Aunt April."

"And the slaughters happening all around—do you listen to the news? Jim-O, I don't know what's gotten into you. Now you're driving all this way on a soaked head. No way you're driving back to that nightclub of yours—you're sleeping here. And that's that."

"Maybe you understand what's going on, because I most certainly don't."

She pulls him in. "Know what? Iced tea. Nothing like hibiscus to shake you out of what's bothering you."

"There's this woman…"

"Finally. One got your heart?"

"I don't want to talk about it."

"Let's talk about something."

He swirls the tea in a china cup. Aunt April's finest, sprigged purple and white, baby petals of lavender. "Why is Buddy messing with me?"

"He's your father."

"He's a fucking slayer."

"Sit."

"Just let me stand."

"You never got closure, that's what you miss when you don't see a funeral."

"The anger and hypocrisy and scariness?"

"There's also love and sorrow."

"I don't need a pity party."

"The hearse, people dressed in black. The scripture. We put her in a coffin, white with silver handles. A padded casket of solid wood."

"Aunt April, stop."

"Topped with lilies speckled white, carnations a blush velvet, chrysanthemums all bicolour—yellow and ruby."

"It was the perfect picture."

"It was overcast, and it drizzled. Lightning, as the coffin lowered."

"It takes more than words."

"If you'd felt the funeral rain, seen the plaque with her name, put a token at her headstone... Maybe, just maybe... If you nibbled the sandwiches... homemade. Custard, bitter orange and spice," she clasps his hand. "That, my Jim-O, all that, would have been closure. But you were a bub. Now listen to me when I say sit."

"Why?"

"You need it for what I'm about to say."

"What can you say? Because maybe I just need to see her grave."

"And you will—it's interstate, where your father lives. I'm just sorry to be the one to tell you this."

"Aunt April, out with it already. There are times I always felt rushed with you, as if you were afraid I might ask questions. I'm beginning to understand it now."

"I didn't want to shake a child's image of his mother."

"What are you talking about?"

"It was better that you hated Buddy."

"Enough with the suspense already!"

"She killed herself, Jim-O. Your mother killed herself."

"What?"

"There. Now you know."

He's quiet a long time. "Then why does Buddy act so guilty?"

"Aren't we all? His womanising. And with a baby, she couldn't take it. Some demons are just bigger than others."

The Truth

The sky weeps tears that the boy-man no longer has.

Neuter's an artist, a double winger. She's winged him. Jim-O.

It's not her intention. She wants, just wants—

This is not closure.

All she wants now, then, tomorrow... She just wants to see him one more time.

It started eons ago. She fell from the skies, pulled her feet and saw a brave little boy with a camouflage hoodie, pull-on chino pants and a stern face. Out on the streets and rejecting the world. But his eyes said different. His hand did too, tight in April's clasp. No, it was April's hand that was tight in his.

April was never long out of reach for Neuter to approach the child. So Neuter spent her panic or rage serial slaying. Now he's grown. The lightning she gets from her barman's voice full of melancholy is far more than the buzz she gets from a kill. She writes on clouds as she soars in drizzle, dangling abstract hearts and futures that'll never be.

She loops and swirls, exits the skies.

Her awakening is communion with a son who's wearing wingbeats for a soul and quotas for love that never happens. He's inked in cypher, shaped like a fist that pounds away distinctions between rage and mourning, one-night stands and the truth of s e l f.

A Deep and Terrible Sadness

YOU'RE A TRAVELLER of the past, present, future. You arrive without land, without name. You have no mission, no affection. Yours is a goading that bares humanity's uncertainties, the kind of fear that breaks mirrors lined on walls. Your mercy is a blanking. The irreal.

Mercy is a place where dingoes grow teeth before snatching bubs from cots, and they wail you invisible. Echoes of their cries dissolve your empathy and you're hardened. You made the decision with clear eyes to stay immune to people.

Yours is a well-travelled road scattered with splintered shells empty of memory, broken jars unfilled with hope. Now you tread along grey asphalt, across the purr and roar of oncoming traffic. You cross to the side, to a sign that says: *2P. 7.30am-8.30pm*. Past an Ezy Mart, *Now Open 24 / 7*, it says. A silver cab crawls past, shadowing a white trades van—electrical or something. Zebra stripes on a red 4WD outside a pillar branded *833*, and an arched entryway to the federal police HQ in a heritage building.

The squeal and halt of a tram that cannot swerve on metal lanes just before a hook turn. You cross the road to a café opposite the copshop, as a ute with a bulbar reverse-parks.

You read the scrawl of an artist's scribble beneath the painting of an ancient one. He's a study with a smudge of forgetting, a twirl of powder-dry—eyes and whiskers that disbelong on the high-commissioned artist's frame. He reminds you of van Gogh, maybe Dante, a voiceless sigh that says fuck off, or get me out of here.

A seated patron in a workman's shirt and a ponytail is tinkering with her smart phone over there. You order a latte, point at a cherry brownie inside the glass case. You choose a mini table that's all black with its mesh chairs, ebony-hued, a good view by a window. You don't mind the light décor in an upside-down calabash of flickering light in flaming gold, but you mind the pebbled plant.

Not much of a view, really:

Safety zone: the end of a tram stop.

Parking: $8 special on a neon sign blinking rich yellow.

Prepare to stop. On the side road.

Keep right, parallel a bicycle lane.

The silver bench by a naked tree might be a sight...

A waitress in a tank top, summer shorts and a graveyard apron delivers your plate beside the plant. You fork a bite, bold red inside the chestnut sheen of the brownie. *Bang, bang*—the barista emptying crushed beans. *Hummm*, the coffee machine. The latte when it arrives (Tank Top) smells roast, cream and melt.

You disturb the white heart on the amber, taste the rich, silk and bittersweet. The second sip is nut, smoke and earth, the third pepper, herb and flower. You wonder if the brownie's petal finish is cranberry or pomegranate, or a tang of hibiscus—nothing sweet.

A low-flying gull flaps its wings too near the glass window. You look at your stained plate and feel the emptiness of conclusion. It awakens an impulse, calls for you to fill the Empty.

You fist your hand, glance around the café. You throw *deep* at the patron and her workman's gear, watch as the smart phone grows in her hand, grows and grows until she can't hold it anymore. She places the colossal phone on the table that groans, tips and slides the device, *crash!* to the floor.

Out the window, a delivery girl tucks on a white helmet, scooters off with a food satchel. A woman in trackies plods into view, and she's pushing a pram. You blow *sadness* at the sleeping bub, and it wakes with a blizzard. Snow and wind crack the windscreen of the ute. It triggers the siren that begins to wail.

You swirl *terrible* at the barista, and the coffee machine turns into a winged manticore—lion-shaped. It gnashes teeth on a man-face, waves

114

quills on a beast tail. It flaps giant bat wings, lunges through the window, over a tram swerving off its rails. Squeals, howls, all deep, sad and terrible, inside the copshop.

Tank Top walks past the patron conversing with the monstrosity of her smart phone. She comes over, reaches to collect your plate stained delish.

How was it?

Very good. Thanks, hey.

Heatwave's a bitch.

Damn right.

The sound of laughter, new patrons at the counter—a couple in a woo. She's fresh-eyed, the float in her poise, half-forward into him... She's unclued to heartbreak.

The girl looks at the pies, looks at him. "What about the tuna mornay?"

"Reckon it's alright." His hand on her back: good contact, solid. He's filled with the right idea until he isn't.

You abandon the mini table, wave at the barista standing there behind the counter with no coffee machine. You step out into the blizzard, pull down your felt hat to cover your ears. Tuck your coat, scarf in a knot. You point a gloved hand towards the skies, levitate and soar to another world.

Deep is here, and here, and here again. An ocean without lines or axes to parallel dimensions. It's impossible to read how high or low the tide. Is it intertidal or littoral? And where in fog's sake is the continental shelf?

Terrible is existential, an abyssal plane where it's relatively flat. You always have it, seek it, mind it, miss it. You are homeless from yourself, an inventory of ambitions you cannot replicate.

Sadness is irrational. It's a trench that shows no gate, just frozen lakes in a topography of salt, kilos and kilos of it. What use is excess saltiness if you're not marine?

There are no coordinates—you've known this all your life. It's a love of intricacies, a dislove of maps stitched like basilisks and manticores in monotone. Contours blur your eyes. But calligraphies pitch narratives of the past, present, future pregnant with the irreal.

Your location is terrible years old.

Your skin peels with sadness.

And no one you know is deep.

Sita and the Fledgling

ONCE UPON a world lives a raven that loves to watch. It's at a time of *the* pandemic[1], so the watching can only be in social or physical distance[2], and in human person-lengths.

Ja is perched on a low-hanging branch, and not standing on a sill, because this is a village, not a town or a city. She's looking at a river of villagers trickling in and out of an old witchdoctor's hut in a slow-moving queue[3].

The witchdoctor's name is Knuckles. He has one blue eye and a black one. He has many totems to commune with the dead. Each idol represents a god, fertility, soil, a good catch, peace, burial, or whatever he wants it to represent. A totem can speak to a lost soul. Most of these souls are still living, which is what fascinates Ja.

About the old witchdoctor's name... It's customary for humans to knuckle their wayward younglings. Perceptions of the old witchdoctor's misshapen noggin suggest that he was exceedingly wayward, and his

---

1   The world is in the throes of grappling with covid-19, and only itinerant folks nomadic across Woop Woop or Turkmenistan may be oblivious of the virus.

2   Whatever you want to call it—anything that makes you feel good about a bad situation, you-know-what-I'm-saying?

3   The queue resembles the long lines you might get at a covid-testing site, especially after a hotspot alert, where waiting times can be as low as 30 minutes and as high as 3 raven days.

mother thoroughly liberal in her application of the knuckles. One assumes that a particular clobbering may have knocked the witchdoctor child to a space between living and dying, which accounts for the blue in his eye. Further speculation may suggest it was the near-death experience that opened the witchdoctor's path for communing with the dead, much as he argues otherwise and brings up miscellaneous facts about universities.

Knuckles has an apprentice, to whom he often says, "No shenanigans." The girl has a deep and terrible sadness about her face. It doesn't matter that she's a tiny one with short tight curls, or that she likes to brush her teeth with a bark-free twig from the savanna grasslands or a carefully shaped sugarcane stem from the back of Knuckle's hut, both of which she chews but only spits with one. It's just as well that she cleans her teeth with whatever instrument of her choosing. If she went 24 hours without brushing, she'd be hosting 100 billion bacteria and an ogre's breath.

It's safe to think that she's an orphan, and stories like Oliver Twist or David Copperfield give good indication of what happens to orphans. The witchdoctor with his height monsters over the girl whose scabs run on her hands, her forehead and her knees—testimony of her lust for clumsiness. She's always running and tripping while obeying the old witchdoctor with her pails, pots and calabashes that keep flying into or out of her hands. Despite the obeyance, Knuckles puts a whistle—literally—to the girl's ear at every turn. He uses it to bid, scurry, snail or terminate the girl's chores. The girl, whose name Ja has learned is Sita, can barely cough or shut an eyelid without that whistle to her ear.

Ja is fascinated with the number of humans falling into the witchdoctor's hut. With all that monstering and whistling, one might expect that he's a frightful being. But villagers keep coming. Most are clad in loin cloth or bark-tree, sometimes an animal skin wrapped around their waists or shoulders. All of them believe in their complaints. When they fall out of the hut, they wear untamed eyes and their clothes are in tatters. They look as if they've just crawled out on knees and elbows from the fangs of an impundulu [*n. eem-poo-ndoo-loo*]. It's a lightning bird—the kind you read about in folklore, and usually guards a witch.

"My husband is cheating on me with a younger woman from a lower caste in the most faraway clan," a villager says.

Knuckles looks at her a long time, and says, "That's so nice."

The woman's downcast eyes hopefully lift. "Really?" she says.

"No. You're a third wheel, then?"

Knuckles collects the woman's gift of a bag of millet. Then he stamps around, banging a talking drum and shaking maracas around the alarmed woman's head. He spits and blows his nose on her shaking knees and says: "In two nights, that scoundrel husband of yours will wake up in the belly of a crocodile, far, far away from you, and it will take him somewhere, or nowhere. When he returns, I can assure that he'll not repeat adultery."

Not knowing what the woman's husband looks like, Ja has no way of confirming the prophesy, insight or treatment. If it's reassuring—she can always check to see if the woman returns to claim her millet.

Ja is rivetted with what the villagers bring as a gift, bribe or payment for the old witchdoctor. Sometimes it's a sack of cassava flour. Sometimes it's yams, arrowroots, sweet potatoes, or slabs of sundried tilapia—these Ja can sniff from a distance, as she can also smell the tiny fish called *omena*, smelly but 'sweet as'.

Ja notices that when the gift is a cockerel, often it's a jet-black bird that's already fearful or enraged, and it flaps or crows. Knuckles knows how to subdue such a bird: he thwacks it on the head, then sanitises his hand with a globule of his own spit[4].

There's one time a woman—arrived from the city—complained about the spitting. "Aw, shut up already," said Knuckles. His eyes bulged from his head and, of course, the woman shut up.

Now Sita—at a whistle—is calming another woman who rushed naked into the boma[5], chased by a clan of men wearing leopard facemasks, and she's wailing, "I am not taking a vaccine!"

---

4   A humanoid mouth has 20 billion bacteria, estimated to reproduce every five hours.

5   The enclosure surrounding the witchdoctor's hut and farm animals.

The husband is trying to placate her, perhaps to save face as he's meant to be the man of the house. "Come home, wife," he's saying. "Please come back with me and we'll talk it out."

"Mfyuuuu, me, never!" cries the wife. "You'll not catch me with trickery."

"Good fun?" says Knuckles to the husband and gives him a big wallop on the ear.

"What was that for?" the man cries.

"I just felt like it."

That's enough to crack the terribly sad girl into a smile.

"And even if you tie me with a rope to drag me," the woman is saying, "I will squeal like you're slaughtering or raping a pig!" She runs so fast, and vanishes from the looking or chasing crowd.

"You're a hunter-gatherer," says Knuckles to the husband. "Stop chasing poor women for vaccinations you don't want to take yourself."

"Where is she?" the man cries.

"I suspect it might help to look below my granary."

Indeed, the woman is there. She screams and pulls her hair as they drag her out. "You vaccinate first, and then me!"

"I'm a bit baffled, to be honest," says Knuckles to the man and his clansmen. "But I will mediate this matter." A witchdoctor can assume many roles, including being a celebrant, performing funeral rites, interceding with the dead, mediating feuds, healing, protecting, educating, advising, and more. The Maji Maji Uprising that happened in the 1800s in German East Africa, for example, had its Kinjekitile Ngwale[6].

Then he looks at the woman. "You idiot," he says. "Contrary to belief, vaccination will not lock up your child-bearing stomach or make you die on the third moon."

The woman squeals, as if someone is killing her. "You are talking like this and you're not even vaccinated. Once you're vaccinated, you'll go completely mad!"

The witchdoctor laughs, and shakes his head.

------

6 The witchdoctor promised the Ngoni people that sacred water would protect black people from white man's bullets. It didn't.

"I will cut my nose and run away to another village, so you'll never find me!" the woman cries.

"You don't need to change your face," says Knuckles. "And your uncle's cows will not lose their calves once you get vaccinated, and touch them. You haven't said this, but you're thinking it."

"Look at that one!" cries the woman. She points at a village idiot wearing goggles, gumboots, a wetsuit and a raincoat. Turns out the idiot is simply a migrant professor from Melbourne on sabbatical, and she's working on a biothermal theorem on the effects of the savanna sunlight on humans.

"And she is not yet vaccinated," howls the woman. "Imagine how worse she'd be if she were vaccinated!"

"I am vaccinated," says the professor.

"See?" shrieks the woman. "A covid shot makes them mad!"

"What's your name?" Knuckles asks the professor.

"Vici, without a *k*."

"That's just dumb. Do you pronounce it Vee-cee?"

The distraction allows the husband and his clansmen to try and muscle the woman back to her children. "Ng'o-oh!" she cries, as she fights them off. "Someone put the crazy out there and they are calling it a pandemic." She knocks her husband with a backhand as if she's possessed by a djinn. "To remind me never to trust your charms, you foolish man, from now on, your name is Covid!"

The husband's consternation is so big that the cockerel he's brought along as a gift or a payment for Knuckles flies out of his hands, and it legs away squawking around the boma. The husband eventually catches the crowing rooster in a floppy tackle that displaces his wraparound.

Eventually, Knuckles rolls his eyes, incants some words, shakes a totem of reeds that represents—what? The woman calms, and agrees to return home if her husband will first take the shot, and then her. Knuckles turns to the clansmen and their leopard skin masks.

"And you fools! A mask is meant to cover your mouth and your nose. It doesn't need holes for breathing."

Ja cocks her head. She's always curious at the calabashes of milk and clubs of honey that folk bring to the old witchdoctor. Rarely—but it happens—a villager rocks up hoisting on their shoulder skewered game (rabbit, warthog or antelope) on a stick, as this young man now.

"I want to be rich."

"Oh, gee. You idiot," says Knuckles. "What does richness look like to you?"

"Cows. Three wives. Many children."

"Well, that skinny hare won't do."

"I also brought you goat stew." His great aunt, who is carrying a pot, steps forward.

"Did you cook it in garlic sauce?" asks the old witchdoctor.

"I did, yes," she says.

"Lots of garlic?"

"Ebooo... yes."

There's the professor and her gumboots, goggles and wet suit. She's making a cameo. "A fine evening to you," she says to no-one in particular.

Ja has two friends, Ze and her twin Sexton[7].

Sometimes you must trust in tradition and throw yourself to that which pertains to words of the elders. You alone cannot fix it. It's customary for ravens to give their chicklings names containing the right consonants. The legacy relates to the idea of names that are easy to caw: Ja! Ze! Bo! Chi! Calling a raven a name like Sexton is simultaneously confusing and just wrong.

Today, Ja, Ze and Sexton are perched on a coconut tree overlooking the witchdoctor's boma. Ze and her twin are also interested in the old witchdoctor, but likely for the wrong reasons. Ja really wants to become an apprentice familiar. One couldn't say the same of Ze and Sexton. What Ze loves to do is sing like a jay, or a goose, or a parrot. What Sexton loves to do is—

Ja is not sure exactly what, especially with a name like Sexton.

A black crow flies close. The trio scream and yell at it, beat their wings until the crow goes out of sight and into the horizon. There's unity at times

---

7   He was born 'Bo', in accord with the tradition of monosyllabic naming of ravens, but later—to impress the ladies—switched to Sexton.

like this. Otherwise, Ja and Ze are always fighting about scraps. They fly at each other, lunge with their bills—Sexton, a bystander. After each fight, he approaches Ze[8], not Ja, and consoles her with a feather preen.

Ja is cross, but not for long. A mother has brought her son to the witchdoctor. The boy has an in-grown nail that looks like the mutated claw of an impundulu.

"Aw, shit," says the old witchdoctor when he sees it.

He scatters spirit water on the woman (not the child), and she flinches.

"It's not the Snowy River," snaps Knuckles. "That's it. Such courage." He gives the mother a paste of camel dung. "Ferment it for seven days, then rub it on the child's claw. If this doesn't fix that revolting thing, I don't think anything will."

Ja, Sexton and Ze collect with a congress of ravens at a roost. Ja is really hoping that today is when they'll take new submissions for expressions of interest to become a familiar. She waits, and waits, but all the congress does is chit, chat, gurgle and grate, as ravens do. So Ja confides in Ze, then Sexton. They open up *a lot*, cawing at each other, even though neither of them has a clue what the other is saying as they warble under twinkling stars.

The rest of the ravens finally quieten and then sleep. The trio sneaks off to nocturnal scouts because humans love barbies at night. They feast on sweetmeats charred on woodfire that flames orange and yellow on baobab wood. Ja, Sexton and Ze flutter from low branches to pale-brown dust, and begin their quest. One strategy that nearly always works is to look, beady-eyed, at the humans as they eat and drink, until they are discomfited enough to chase the ravens and throw at them scraps. If this isn't ravenhood, what is?

They return, gorged, to find that the old witchdoctor has a night visitor.

"This one fell off a mango tree," says a boy's mother, "and he's keeping us awake with his crying."

---

8   Twins are known to share a particularly intense bond that is powerful and unique. It may include telepathy, own language, and all manner of physical, emotional or spiritual affiliation.

"Did you bring a little sumthn, sumthn?" Knuckles looks at the mother.

She hands over a wobbly sack that has snarling coming out of it. Knuckles peers in quickly and snaps his face out of the opening. He ties the burlap strings.

"Good. I hate to see people hurt." He whacks the boy hard on the shoulder, which throws the lad to the ground. Knuckles sits on him and forces the shoulder back in place. The boy is crying. His mother is crying. Knuckles is crying... which gives the trio of ravens ample time to peck open the strings of the wobbling sack.

They steal in and immediately hop out with throaty kraas! and in flight from a terribly angry cat. Finally, safe on a coconut tree.

Some of Knuckles' night visitors have been patiently waiting since morning in a queue outside the hut. Tired, they are game. Ja, Sexton and Ze snatch the moment. They fly at folks' faces, flapping their wings, and Kraa! startle them. The villagers drop baskets filled to the brim with delicious goodness that the ravens swiftly but thoroughly pirate. Once Ja stumbled upon freshly-steamed banana coated with a fry of bovine[9] intestines. Please don't think that being opportunist makes ravenhood evil: a raven's got to live. Given half a chance with those humans, Ja knows she'd be bones and a broth inside a clay pot.

Before retiring back to the roost, Ja, Sexton and Ze listen to a young man's complaint. "My neighbour is bewitching my goats—I want to counter his attack with a protecting potion."

"Mindboggling," says Knuckles, and accepts the full pot of millet beer from the man's hands. He frightens the poor man half out of his wits with ritual, then says:

"Crack the eggs of a spotless hen and bring me the yolks. Of course, I will eat them. Keep the shells and dry them under a morning sun on the roof of a virgin granary that no-one has defiled. Do not visit with your wife for seven days, then take the shells and put them upside down around your hut."

---

9   Bovine is just a manner of speaking, as they were large enough to be a cow's or a bull's intestines, but it could well have been an alpaca's or a grandfather goat's, you-know-what-I'm-saying?

"If I do all this," says the man, "It will bring protection?"

"I sure hope so! But, first, use antibacterial hand sanitiser. Get hospital grade: No rinse, no fuss. Ninety-nine percent of germs—poof! Just like that."[10]

Dawn breaks. The trio is a duo. Neither Ja nor Sexton know what's happened to Ze.

And Sexton is acting funny, not as in haha. He's croaking and rasping, bowing in a manner that's unfamiliar to Ja and leaves her perplexed. She gets it when his grating shifts to soft cooing, bowing and nuzzling. She screams at him and nuzzles him back, as he softly sings.

Perched on a branch, they trade myths, misconceptions, judgements and greed. A raven's water hardly changes into wine, but she can pilfer from a shaded balcony up, up on a skyscraper. Only it's a village, no towers here. Just slinking snakes, ripe durians and archetypes to misinterpret, the roles only temporary.

Sexton is a bit of a slow starter—it's as if he needs a claw up his butt[11] to jolt him to action. His pickup-line and everything-line is a gargle that sounds like, *Not sixty percent*. Ja hopes she's heard it wrong. That what he barks when he swells his neck, rattles his throat and looks into her soul is: *You seem perfect*.

They wrestle with beaks and twigs, nips and claws, as if they are one. It's a wooing of its kind, Sexton rubbing against her all frisky and croaking. He perches on top of her, rubbing and gargling, until she can't hold the urgency any longer and finally moves for him her tail feathers[12]. In the heart of copulation, Ja sees a raven that looks like Ze sitting on the windowsill—indeed, suddenly there's a sill—right there, outside the

---

10   By now you're wondering what's happened to Sita and her deep and terrible sadness. Patience, she's coming. There's going to be a plot twist.

11   Literally, this is a *cloaca*.

12   A female raven moves her tail feathers to expose her *cloaca*—the same one that poos; not very sexy in use and sound, you-know-what-I'm-saying? The male arches his back and rubs against her, depositing his sperm from his own *cloaca* (not a penis) to fertilise the egg.

old witchdoctor's hut. But she's enamoured in a woo and entwined in amorousness. She throws her heart wide open, and wakes on a branch to find herself in a map of absence.

The morning has pickpocketed her trust, and nothing looks like her lover. Sure, Sexton is there, and he's approaching for what he hopes might be another... But Ja is thinking about her future, precisely what is the future that holds her name? Suddenly she realises that she likes Jacee. She doesn't know where the name has come from but she really, really likes it.

She also chooses to consider—sixty percent of anything is better than minus percent. Her mind is prowling and it's seeking a perfect answer with no residue of quiet groaning. Reality is the branch of a leaf that doesn't exist, and trying to figure it out is a dawn too far, she's lucky if she or the gatekeepers can locate half a start.

As she contemplates what future a name like Jacee might hold for her, Sexton grates, gurgles and screams something that sounds like, *I could have sworn there was a connection.* She shrinks from his touch, the memory of it alien. The rising sun is appalled at Ja's gaze, the sound of her silence resounding unabridged: It's you, not me.

She swoops down from the coconut tree and hops to the old witchdoctor's boma. She makes a noise, a godawful din, kraa! kraaing! as she flaps her wings at the hut's door made of blackwood, not mahogany. Inside, from behind the door, she hears Knuckles bark: "No shenanigans!"

Then the door snaps open and the girl, Sita, tumbles out with flying knees and a pail. She's also holding seven fishing rods and trips, ooof! her foot catching on one rod. She picks herself from the dirt and hobble-runs all the way to the creek that's drying up.

The old witchdoctor storms to the doorway and sees Ja.

"What do you want?"

"I..." Ja opens her mouth to caw some more.

Knuckles takes one look at her tail feathers that have moved and says, "Bloody awful. Youse been shagged."

"But I..."

"I only take virgin ravens, male or female, to become my familiar."

"But I..."

"You see that one," he points at Ze on the windowsill still. "She's a virgin but is no bloody good. Youse a both no bloody good."

He slams the blackwood, not mahogany, door snap! shut on her face.

Up on the roost, Sexton is nowhere in sight. Ja finally brings herself to ask Ze, who gargles something like he's left for another territory.

Ja looks down in moroseness, at the old witchdoctor's morning queue of visitors.

"My foolish daughter will not accept marriage to Obindi," a father says, "and I have already taken his cows for dowry."

"Imbecilic," says Knuckles. "Did you bring a little sumthn, sumthn?"

The man hands the old witchdoctor a rope at the end of which is a billy goat.

"Good. I wouldn't accept marriage to a man named Obindi, either," says Knuckles. He makes the man run around the boma seven times in a sprint. "Faster!" The man is huffing and puffing when the old witchdoctor offers him treatment: "Take three cows that have white patches on the face. Sell one, give me one, and slaughter one—make sure you invite me to the feast."

The man raises his brows.

"What? It is what it is," says Knuckles. "Cost me a bit, you know— they don't offer witchdoctoring at common universities. I had to go to Harvard."

"You want a whole cow?" the man sputters.

"You're welcome to bring a quarter cow, as long as it's alive."

When the man returns with the cow for Knuckles, the old witchdoctor tells him, "You're a bloody idiot. Telling you anything will go nowhere— still, I'll say it. The literacy rate of a female of 15 years and over is... I don't remember what it is. Frankly, I have no idea. But it's low in the village, alright? Putting a child to grade 6 is not giving her a chance. So stop marrying your girls to impotent oldies and educate them as if it were an investment, because it is."

"How is schooling a girl an investment?"

"Try it and you'll see. She'll come back from the city to the village as a teacher or a doctor."

"I don't need a doctor or a teacher other than you," says the man, and lays a hand on the old witchdoctor's cloak.

Knuckles brushes him off. "I'm gutted by your idiocy."

"What shall I do about the dowry?"

"Give it back to Obindi."

"But I'm short three cows."

"Good for you!" says Knuckles.

"How?"

"I mean *shame* on you. Find replacement cows quickly, or I'll fine you with a rather large bull. Serves you right for misdirection and ill-thinking towards young girls."

The professor whose name is Vici without a *k* makes a cameo. "Adelaide is the third most liveable city in the world," she says. "It's in the latest Economic Intelligence Unit report. Take your daughter to Adelaide."

"Really?" the man says, with a glimmer of hope.

"Yes," the professor says. "But Geelong is my footy team[13]. Trounced the West Coast Eagles by... I can't remember by how many points, just a lot. Go Cats!"

Life happens, and Ja is miserable. Jacee is stupid. What raven in the roost or skies would ever want a name like Jacee? She's felt bloated for three days. On the fourth, she lays a single egg. Seriously. One. What took several attempts, copulating many times through the night[14], the ingrate Sexton managed to fertilise only one egg. Not three or four or five as usual in a raven's clutch.

Sexton is still nowhere in sight. What Ja believed was a love match was no more than a rub of feathers and ugly-cry wooing, and now he has abandoned Ja to single parenthood[15]. It's Ze who feeds Ja worms,

---

13   She's talking about Aussie rules, which is Australian football. Whatever you do, please don't try to understand it, just enjoy the bloody game.

14   During mating, ravens have sex *a lot*—perhaps it's for pleasure, or to assure the birds of a bigger chance of fertilisation.

15   Ravens mate for life, but sometimes a male is known to juggle two females in adjacent villages or territories.

maize seeds, roadkill (it's mostly a kill from bicycles and one-wheelers), eggshells, grasses and what humans call refuse. The incubation takes a whole 21 days, and Ja considers taking on Ze as a mate. But she too buggers off soon as the egg cracks and a hairless chickling that looks like the regurgitate of an impundulu breaks out hungry.

Ja's heart sinks. It takes two parents, not one, to feed starving chicklings. Baby ravens make a lot of noise, and tell parent ravens just how deeply hungry they are. And this one is a greedy one, ungrateful as its father. It loves grains—mostly rice and sorghum, fruits—a penchant for mango, durian, tangerine and pineapple, but farts with coconut shaving. It also enjoys rain termites—but there's not much rain— eggshells, peanuts and shreds of the foul-smelling omena fish.

It needs two parents, not one, and often to console each other. Ja curses Sexton, and Ze, and suddenly remembers how Ze sat on the old witchdoctor's windowsill as her twin distracted Ja. It finally dawns on her. She understands too late, the deceit sharp in her head. It was all a trick, one that would succeed in making sure Ja could never achieve her quest of wanting to be a familiar bird for the old witchdoctor.

She flies down to the windowsill and looks glumly inside the old witchdoctor's hut and its totems of rooster heads, spearheads and amulets.

A visitor to Knuckles' hut is all covered in cowshit. "Help me!" the woman says. "My only cow is calving wrong!"

"You reckon?" says the witchdoctor. He does his ritual of jumping and shouting, today wearing only a sisal skirt and cowrie shells. Then he says, "Cover the cow's eyes with a wet black cloth soaked in menstrual blood. Wait as she pushes, until she reaches the seventh contraction from the first time you start counting, and put over her eyes the umbilical cord of a fresh stillborn."

"A stillborn what?"

"A stillborn anything."

"And this will save my cow?"

"It will give her a glimpse of where motherhood might go if she doesn't push right."

Today Ja is not at the windowsill. She looks from the tree as the door of the hut opens. Sita falls out running for the river with a pail. Ja waits, waits, until her timing is impeccable. She nudges the chick from the stick nest just as the girl reaches below the coconut tree, but the girl's reflexes are flawless. She catches the screaming[16] chick as it falls—how Sita does this with the running and a pail is any raven's guess.

Ja watches as the girl hops onto the base of the tree, grips it with her bare hands and grope-climbs it, her legs in an inward grip. Her knees are all frogged, but she pushes up and up the tree, until she reaches the right tapered leaflet along which the nest is nestled. Still clutching the tree with her thighs, Sita delicately pulls the petrified chick from the pocket of her tunic.

"Oh, there you are," she says, and delicately slots the unfeathered chick[17] back next to Ja, at whom she wags a finger. "Bad mother!"

Sita frogs down the way she came but slips half-way down and crashes, face down in a scatter. Her feet and heels are all cut, her palms bruised, but she collects her pail and races off to the drying creek, humming, to be back on time for an ear clout, a whistle and the words, "No shenanigans."

"That was deliberate," screams the chickling at Ja. Well, that is what it sounds like.

"Take one for the team," says Ja.

She decides, to spite Sexton, on a name: Chi.

"Shots in a row," says the professor to no-one in particular. It's another cameo appearance.

Ja deems the nab of the plummeting chickling a lucky first. But the girl Sita never misses the catch. Or fails to climb the tree. Do you know how hard it is to climb a coconut tree? Today she clumsy-topples on the way down, and lands on her ribs. She gasps, short of breath[18]. Then she picks

---

16   A raven screams when it's pooing, wooing or gleeful, and it's possible the chickling was undertaking all three.

17   A raven chick takes 14 days for feathers to emerge. It takes 35-36 days for the chick to fully feather.

18   A symptom of covid but, in this case, the girl is simply stretched.

her pail and fishing rods and clips her foot on a protruding grass as she runs to the creek.

As the girl races back with muddy water dripping down her head, Ja nudges Chi off the nest. The second catch is even better, but the water wobbles dangerously before balancing on the girl's head.

"Thinking of a nice ball moment," smiles the professor, taking off her goggles. "Reminds me of Dangerfield's timeless mark, right up there." She's wearing a dreamy look on her face. "And that pass to Hawkie... You don't see much like it these days."

The girl ponders for a moment what to do with the pail of water, or Chi who is screaming in her hands. She tilts the water and abandons the pail, climbs the tree and secures the chickling back in the nest, even though it's harder to climb a coconut tree when one is wet.

Ja watches, perplexed, as Sita picks her pail and trips on a pebble in her race to the creek for a scoop of new water. She contemplates how Sita's run might be slicker if the village had soft, green savanna grass—the kind you find in the wet season—rolling at her feet. But there's none of that here. The girl is clumsy all the way and back with her pail, falling and tripping in uneven gait.

The girl, Sita, has improved when it comes to saving Chi from a topple. Today, she does a little shimmy with her body, while holding a full pail in her hand. She's on the way back from the creek. As Ja jolts the chickling, Sita does a 'headie', the head-wobble kind of move she does when she balances a pot. She catches Chi with the top of her head, flicks the chick down to her foot, and swings. Chi flies beautifully, safe all the way up in an arc, and rolls back into the nest.

Incredible. It's as if, all her life, Sita's goal or destiny is to arrive at a perfect catch right under a coconut tree, flawless in her execution, even though she looks deeply, terribly sad.

"Knows how to do it," says the professor in another five minutes of fame. "A swing-back footy, that's what."

Ja contemplates another tree, but what's harder to climb than a coconut tree? There's a thorn tree, but that would just be mean. Given the girl's proclivity to clumsiness, imagine her bouncing in a fall between branches. It would also entail Ja having to hoist with her beak and fly a whole nest and its plump Chi all the way to a brand new tree—metaphorically speaking, as it wouldn't be a new tree, simply another one.

The girl continues to leap over the top of her head at impossible heights. She even jumps backwards and in slow motion, as if she has eyes at the back of her head, and her fingers snap up high to catch Chi. One time she backfoots in a left-foot flyer at an angle that doesn't look good yet perfect-lands the chick, unscathed, but screaming, straight through the leaves and neatly into the nest.

"Perfect curl around the ball," the professor whose name is Vici without a *k* says.

And, as it happens with repeat near-crashing, Chi grows increasingly confident. The chick's ear-splitting screech down the tree gets small, smaller, and then non-existent. It turns into a gleeful cry or gargle, something that sounds a bit like "Sweet contact!"

Nevertheless, each time the girl gets all clumsy after she has delivered the chickling, now partially feathered and a tad good-looking. Today she falls on her ribs again and hobbles off with her pail and seven calabashes to the creek.

Ja is nonplussed. It's a stalemate of fall and catch with a girl who makes a catch out of nothing. It doesn't help that Chi looks Ja in the eye and says, "I'm still young[19]."

Well, that's what it sounds like, hard to tell with croaks and garbles.

"I am not trying to kill you," says Ja simply.

She scratches her beak in bafflement. She's running out of time. In 35 days, the chick will start learning how to fly, then it will leave the nest, but come back to it. In 3-4 months, Chi will leave the nest and never come back. It's the stage where young ravens leave their parents. Parent, in this case.

Ja doesn't know how to explain that she, honestly, hasn't been trying to kill her chick, despite the scoundrel of Sexton and his Ze. It's all part

---

19   A raven has the lifespan of 10-15 years. This one is now feathered, and it usually takes 35-36 days for a chick to fully feather.

of a strategy. And time is racing. Once Chi leaves the nest, that's the end of non-explaining.

Ja feels a little better that she's not the only one who'll be abandoned. Because she's witnessing a wailing woman who has fallen into the boma and is outside the hut door that's made of blackwood, not mahogany.

"You have sumthn, sumthn?" Knuckles looks at her.

She hands him a burlap sack, and it's all bloodied.

"Good. What can I do for you?"

"I want Uvundindi to love me, but he is enamoured with Chief Ikelezi's daughter!"

"What a juvenile thing."

The woman looks up hopefully.

"Are you for real?" asks Knuckles.

She hangs her head. "Already she has nine suitors and I have none," she says.

"Go home," says Knuckles. "Put ochre on your face and do not wash for seven nights straight. Cook a flat bread over sandstone hearthstones and sit on it with bare buttocks. Take this oil and put it on the fingers of Uvundindi's thatch on the roof," he gives her a potion. "Once you have smeared it, apply it all the way in droplets, stopping to chant every seven steps, from his hut to yours."

"Why do I have to spill droplets of potion on the dusty path away from his hut until I reach mine?"

"It will lure him to your kitchen where you'll serve him the buttocked bread."

"It will work?"

"Let's put it like this. He will love you to the grave[20]."

Ja doesn't know when the congress of ravens will next be taking applications for apprenticeship as a familiar bird to a witchdoctor. She missed her chance because of an otherwise engagement that had two names on it. Ze did not even go ahead to become a familiar herself.

---

20   Knuckles did not specify whose grave he meant.

Sure, she could sing like a jay, or a goose, or a parrot—that didn't make her familiar material, as Knuckles has testified, which makes the twins' deception worse. Their betrayal was of a manner that breached ravenhood, even though ravens didn't really do hoods.

"I slept with a virgin so that covid will go away," Chief Ikelezi is saying.

"Did you bring a little sumthn, sumthn?" Knuckles asks, and accepts the gift of a giant drum made of the underbelly of an ostrich. He looks up. "The virgin. Was it a girl or a goat?"

"Ebooh! It was a girl."

Knuckles enters his hut and comes out of it with a spear.

Chief Ikelezi squeaks.

That's enough to crack the terribly sad girl whose name is Sita, and she's an apprentice, into a smile.

But the spear is simply for the chief to hold upright while seated on the dirt ground and facing the sun at an angle that corresponds with the corner of his left eye, while the witchdoctor pounds the back of the chief's head with a punchbag made of seven-day-old fishtails.

Ja can smell them from her tree. Chi can too, screaming for food, until the chief looks up at the coconut tree.

"Eyes up front," barks Knuckles.

At this exact time, the professor looks up from her notes, and peers through her goggles at the chief sat aground and holding a spear. "Now that's really dangerous," she says. "In footy, we call that holding the ball."

"Really?" says the chief.

"It will test you," the professor says, and marches off with her galoshes and wet suit.

Knuckles is done with the spear-holding and fish-tail-clobbering ritual. "Life for gold," he says to the chief. "Not many people can sit through that shit, but you did."

"Is that all?"

"Eat the brains of a tilapia seven nights in a row."

"Will it cure my covid?"

"No. But it will take stupidity from your head and grow you some fish brains."

"I am the chief!"

"And zero-brained. I would advise you to get onto the next plane to Nincompoopland."

The virgin that chief Ikelezi defiled is carried to the boma. She has a dry cough, the shakes and a temperature.

"And Sydney!' cries the professor whose name is Vici, without a *k*. It's yet another cameo appearance into a story in which she doesn't belong. "All those Delta infections, it's a horror show."

Knuckles looks at the virgin's mother and kindly says, "What you need is the poop of a raven chick, like that one up the coconut tree over there." He points upwards at Ja's nest.

"Sita, no shenanigans!" The girl trips from a chore and falls at the old witchdoctor's feet. "Climb that coconut tree and grab the chickling."

Ja looks at Chi. "You know I love you?" she says.

Chi looks back at her, and says kraa! kraa! warble, warble.

The girl leaps at the tree from the base, frog-climbs it beautifully. She reaches into the nest and gently extracts Chi, who hops into her hands. The girl shimmies down the tree perfectly, one handed. She flies back to the old witchdoctor's boma without falling or tripping.

This how Chi winds up as a familiar bird. Did I tell you Chi's a she?

She is now perched, a constant companion, on Sita's shoulder. This was all part of Ja's strategy.

"The umpire says no," cries the professor from a distance. The sabbatical is nearing its end and, soon, she must return to Melbourne. But there's a limited quota for international arrivals into Australia, and the professor will be lucky to make the cut. If she does, she'll have to do hotel quarantine for 14 days, and that whole process is bungled. So she might end up becoming a super-spreader, causing more community consternation, and yet another lockdown for Victoria as a result of concern about new cases, even if they are five.

Ja has been experiencing a loss of taste, and is a little worried. But perhaps it's PTSD after the trauma of everything she has been through, even if it's a happy ending. She can't make it as a familiar, but her fledgling can.

This is great news. But Ja has just learnt something new that's unsettling. What she understood was a call for apprenticeship as a familiar bird to a witchdoctor—in which she failed to qualify because she was with chick and confined to a nest—came out of a committee, not a congress of ravens. The congress is, in fact, just a grouping of ravens, not a legislative body of federal government.

"Don't zip when others zap," cries the professor, on her way to hotel quarantine.

In a new case alert, the old witchdoctor's hut has been declared an exposure site. Sorry, that's misinformation—you might as well believe that a gnat can copulate with a raven. The true thing is that Knuckles' boma has become a pop-up vaccine centre, and it's Knuckles who is administering it. The first woman in the story, her husband and his clansmen, all wearing leopard-skinned facemasks covering their mouths and noses, are standing in a queue.

Knuckles declines their gifts of calabashes, sacks or a live or dead thing tethered at the end of a rope. "It's on me," he says. "This one is free." He blows a whistle at Sita, the girl who is his apprentice. He says, "No shenanigans! Look at these people. I want you to put them in a row."

Sita complies, and Chi the fledgeling helps, croaking, rasping, gurgling and screaming at the village folk, caught up in a fighting match of 'Me, first', all wanting to take the vaccine quickly. What's happened to change their minds is that this part of the world is suffering an alarming second wave of viral infections. Seeing masses of hospitalisations and folk dying, or hearing tell of it, is enough to temporarily inhibit the superstition of the staunchest believer, and villagers have accepted white people medicine for now.

Knuckles glares, mostly with his blue eye. He halts the villagers' shoving and squabbling with a hand.

"There's enough for all of you."

"Even me?" Ja nears.

"Even you," says the old witchdoctor.

"Is the vaccine Raveneca?"

"It's not Raveneca, or any eneca."

"Is it Rizer?"

"Not even a Roson or Roson. Take what is locally available or raven off."

The shot doesn't hurt. The old witchdoctor even allows Ja to rest a little in his hut, and beak his many totems that commune with the dead. But a witchdoctor can only take so much, especially this one, and he promptly shoos her when she beaks into a calabash of sorghum beer. Kraa! she's a bit tipsy from fermented sorghum or the shot.

Occasionally, you will see a tight-haired orphan girl with a deep and terrible sadness about her face, and she's running around, tripping and falling, with a baby raven perched on her shoulder. She might also be holding a pail, a calabash, seven fishing rods for the sake of it. Sometimes she forgets and runs back for more water when the witchdoctor doesn't need any. He whistles and barks, "No shenanigans." The smile on her face is beatific.

Still nothing of Sexton, but word has it that he's flown across the oceans to a place called Wagga Wagga or Woop Woop. As if Ja cares.

So this is the story of Ja the raven that loves to watch, how she got conned by a Casanova named Sexton, but her fledgling still became a familiar to an old witchdoctor named Knuckles.

Fire Fall on Them

THE LIBRARIAN'S eyes are a gale. She's not Lily, delicate Lily, a white blossom who skips your heartbeat. Lily, whose face is the shape of a floret, whose eyes remind you of a butterfly on a petal against a soft cerulean canvas. Lily, the picture of elegance, serenity. Fourth-year Lily, student librarian. You like how she flirts with you a little, lets you help her up a ladder to fetch your favourite book, any book—it's your favourite when Lily touches it—because library rules say only a librarian can climb a ladder to reach a shelf. She fills you with a sweet disquiet in the sombre sandstone and quartzite walls of the library. Not to make light of it but you'd tap her in a minute...

She's totally your type, but you know you're not hers. She prefers high-rollers like Jules and Pal, cruising on six-cylindered sports cars with turbo grunt, while you hotfoot it from home and back. You didn't ask to be born without a gilded spoon in your mouth, and it gets you sore sometimes, but hey... Nothing you can do to change where, how or why you're born. And first-year students don't get that lucky.

St Jude's squats in a leafy suburb rolling in money. Cake houses security-walled to the nth, you can barely see the tip of a chimney, and the houses are tiered. It's the kind of wealth that stays in the family, streets so clean you can eat off them with a fork. Heck, the baker gives you bubbles, as in champagne not soapsuds, while you wait for white truffle, blue pheasant or foie gras pies. The butcher doesn't mess you around either. Neat cuts so red and lean, even the Kobe cow softened with operetta and reflexology doesn't know how good a life it had.

Carmille Cabeyo, this librarian's badge says. She looks wrong, and it's not because she's not a looker. Yeah, she's not a looker. Her left eye's bigger than the right. Her nose is a chin—that's just unlucky. So she's all wrong. You can't tell if she's a phantom or has part-blood apparition ancestry. She looks at you above the rim of her pushed-down spectacles in a way that tells you to present your student ID. And you do.

You don't mind libraries, really, you don't. But today, you mind this one very much. What you feel is an active dislike—because what kind of teacher imposes a library as a punishment?

Sure, you'd called Miss Jumanne a cunt. She was acting like one. Not in a sexual way, no. With those wilderness eyes and that nest of hair, she's not your type. It doesn't matter that she's a migrant who refuses to assimilate. Afro bangs and animal-print batiks. Puffed-up sleeves. Lions, gazelles, giraffes—she likes inhabiting them as prints on her clothes. Even crocs, as in gobbler riverside ones, not shoes. You've had the hots for refugee types before, yeah, that new caramel-skin in 1B—from north or north-east, some mouthful country with an 'e' or an 'i' in it. Makes second- and third-years *trip* like they've seen a cherub, drooling and sitting through boring shit like netball to watch her bounce her bits. Yeah, that one. She's foie gras, edible gold.

If Miss Jumanne has any bits, they're well hidden. The batiks don't add to the list of things you dislike about Miss Jumanne. She eggs you how she talks, each word a drip of condescending. She has this way of saying, or non-saying—it reminds you of your irascible mother. The guilts. You feel naughty, as in bad, not cheeky. Your mama pulls her nose when she enters your room with a knuckle knock. Doesn't give you time to get ready. Pokes her head and you feel all bad, knowing that your room is all bad, the way she looks at your undies, your jackets, your T-shirts all crumpled and bad over an empty soda tinnie you crushed and practice-threw at the swivel chair you swiped from your mother's home office. Your mother doesn't say anything but it's there in her eyes and you know she knows you feel bad. As if she wants you to feel a deep and terrible sadness, but you don't.

Sometimes she looks up at the ceiling, searching for a word from the Lord, a sign that maybe he's heard her prayer or petition.

When she looks back at you, you know what she's thinking, and they're words she cannot say out loud. How she should have squeezed her legs when you were coming out, but it was the Lord's will and you're the focken cross she must live with. Your mother is there but you don't feel like there's a parent. She's been missing from the day you were born. You're not sure how you feel about your mother. Whatever it is, it's not good.

Miss Jumanne also reminds you somewhat of Auntie Alice. You don't know how she's your auntie, cos she's not your mother's sister, cousin, or anything close like that, but she behaves in your house as if she's a conjoined twin. Never leaves your mother's side, throws her weight around—she's in front of your face all the time. Plonks herself with a sigh on the sofa and makes you watch the bitch magistrate with a wig on reality TV, the one who acts all mighty hearing cases, wearing her crow face and black plumes for a fake audience and her sheriff. You don't like how Auntie Alice caws her glee, "Sweet name of Jesus, fire fall on them!" when the magistrate bangs a gavel and barks, "This ruling is final," and your mother forgets to be all grumpy, laughs along and says, "Yes, Lord."

Miss Jumanne reminds you a little of Grandma—the mother of a father you never knew. She lives remote in a place called Woodend. What you don't understand is this: why can't Grandma stay like he did—away? She's all chatty like a cockatoo, wears this unshakeable scent of toilet freshener and brings those awful scones that look and taste like a bone the dog has licked, any dog, a drooly one mostly. But she's got brass and it pays for St Jude's.

Shit had to come to a head with Miss Jumanne, didn't it? You love books and literature, but how are stories about slaps or keeping souls or book thieves... classics?

"I expect you to participate in my class," Miss Jumanne said in that flowing accent of hers, almost sing-song like, some tribal ditty. Not that you've heard any such lilt, or that she's from anywhere close to anything you know, but still. "Stu, hear what I said?"

Finally, you looked up from your comic—*IT Guy*'s dope.

Doesn't cost much when you get the latest mag from the corner shop with a bloke named Bob who cuts you a deal. You can begin reading before you reach the street that turns sharp and away from the normal people-land and into the shiny school suburb. You'd like to learn how to write and draw like the *IT Guy* artist. Satire and fock-you in rib-tickler sticks and circles. Callouts with a lot of wise in them.

Miss Jumanne looked at you like she didn't get the wise in comics, so you said, "What's the big deal?"

"Learning is an opportunity your generation needs to appreciate," she said.

"The heck you mean?"

"I need you to sanitise your language."

The class tittered. Your mates Jules and Pal wore faces that were not, *What are you, retarded?* Or *That's bad.* But rather, *That's dope.* Only a few dolls like that Holy May with her designer bangs gave you a stunned stare that said, *You're screwed, mate.*

They're decent kids from parents who can throw three or four siblings in a school that asks for five digits per student per term. That kind of school where you learn to row, fence and ride ponies for focken polo or equestrian. They don't do shit like triathlons or footy, where— right foot snap—you put a boot to the ball and let it rip, a clean slice through the sticks as peeps cheer. Sure, there's hockey, but it's all posh, polite clapping, no-one helping themselves to a roar, because a goal. The cafeteria serves bird's nest soup and abalone, but you eat grandma's scones. Understandably, you have anger, a lot of it, that's a fact, and it likes coming out in Miss Jumanne's class.

"Life's a risk," you said, more to Holy May than to the teacher.

"Be part of this class to stay in it," said Miss Jumanne.

"Why?"

"Shall I speak to your mother again?"

"What? No!"

"Then stop mucking around—"

"That's nice—"

"And, right now, take your disinterest elsewhere—"

"That's just a cunt—"

"I'm sorry?" she said.

"Nothing," you said.

If Auntie Alice were here, she'd be doing that sweet name of Jesus shit. But Miss Jumanne just said, "Stand up right now, Stu Joseph Reynolds. Go to the library at once."

"But why?"

"You're going to research great women in history." She was pissed, like real pissed, and that's a beaut, but her voice was calm. "What I need from you is an essay, round inch margins, five A4 pages single-sided, double-spaced, in size 12 Serif font, and I need it by lunchtime."

You blew her a kiss. "I'll see you soon."

You don't know why you said this. To be cool? It's good as. Every focken kid in the classroom looked at you like you were focken Thor.

You'd have soared on top of the world, on the tip of Mount Olympus. But there was this storm in Miss Jumanne's eyes, a real storm, whirly swirly foggy white inside, and it had heat coming from it. Who knew a refugee's journey, how they got to wherever they got? You'd awakened something in Miss Jumanne, and it wasn't good. You felt overheated and touched your forehead, then your neck, and the storm in those eyes made you feel how your mother makes you feel, just hundreds of times worse.

Despite the eyes, Miss Jumanne was smiling, calm to the class, but that look was a curse.

So today you dislike both the library and the punishment—you might not have minded either too much if it had a Lily in it, but there's gale-eyed Carmille Cabeyo. You walked all the way along the hall and out past the gym and netball court in its three equal parts and two goals, past the car park lit with gleamers, the kind of shit rich kids drive, and you're talking mercs, jags, lambors and hypersports, you walking, walking all that way for a goggle-eyed, chin-for-a-nose library bitch named Carmille Cabeyo. Cos that's who you found.

The sandstone and quartzite building was probably a teacher's house back then. It has arched windows and thick pillars, one painted ceiling in the Harold Holt microfiche room, but it's no bibliotheca or a Library of Congress worth centuries of artefacts.

You browse the shelves for books that might be about great women in history, but where do you start when your mother's a bitch, your auntie's a bitch, your grandma's a bitch, your teacher's a bitch—not really a cunt—and there's no role model for you to learn from? You run a hand across books and periodicals, look at others high up on gilded shelves that need a ladder, but there's no way you're asking some Carmille Cabeyo bitch to climb up on your behalf, so you can look up her skirt as you totally would for Lily.

What you discover as you browse is that there are a lot of books by men about men, some by women but also about men, books and books of them, microfilms, audiobooks, blue rays and ebooks. Pawing, then poring through them makes you wonder where the fock those great women are when you need them.

Your desk is polished elm, heartwood coloured, a reddish-brown. Its ring pattern interlocks with the wood grain in a course texture, still it's nothing like sitting in a reading room of a soft-lit exhibit museum, glass-shelved, coffer-ceilinged, tier-storeyed, like you see protagonists do in movies. A library is for one to browse the shelves for books, sit, read and study, borrow something with a due date, not for punishment!

If only there were tens or hundreds of dedicated staff on hand to help you in this impossible quest to uncover—not just one—10 great women! But there's just Carmille Cabeyo. You glance at the main desk, scowl at the librarian who doesn't say a word, just looks at you above the rim of her pushed-down spectacles in a way that tells your exasperation to hush.

You feel the heat in that look as if Camille Cabeyo's bitch-eyes are flamethrowers.

The room's temperature suddenly soars, and your head is bursting. An echo slips off Cabeyo's heated gaze as you pick a book from your pile. You don't belong here. Carmille Cabeyo doesn't belong here. The damn book doesn't belong here. The thrum of its text rocks you to a dream

144

place, arms wrapped around yourself on a cloud humping in the tempest of the librarian's stare.

You don't know if this is hallucination, purgatory, or the curse of juju. You rouse to more books beneath a catacomb of floorboards: picture books, a thesaurus, Mary Shelley's *Frankenstein* and is that *Gulliver's Travels*? What was once a building is now a cave or an alley, everything plunged in a gobbling darkness. But each book shimmers its title. That one there has a neon of Flaubert's bird. What's this? *Windmill of the Gods*. That's not the librarian—it's a question in your head, not a statement. There's a lot of her prowling in many selves and complex shadows no-one wants to speak of—do you remember how she was when you entered the library? She looks... *It looks* like what ate Carmille Cabeyo, and it's galloping towards you.

Vertigo. Agoraphobia. A waft of lilac and jasmine, as in colour, indigo and violet whirls in the grave-lit room. Embossed Latin on a hand-crafted book in double dragon leather tears out in flames. A wood-carved journal twinkles, tries to change its script in a thimble of light. But the shelf is burning, hot as the lips of a Satanized nymph who gives you nightmares, orgasms and suffocations right before you wake, or fall off a question-mark staged for yourself.

But who are you? You lose your identity as your mother slits your throat and you resurrect with hunger, such hunger, a new-born vampire, or perhaps a tragic monster that doesn't feel like a demon, just full of heart and soul, yet so many zeroes, each of them a noose.

How many times can you die?

You leap onto a bus, find yourself in a cell walled with newspapers. Your muscles are falling. Your stomach is melting. Your heart is burning, burning. So thirsty... is this evolution? You see blue death in a jungle lit with calling apes, all real and multi-limbed and their cries splatter manuscripts: crimson, noir and sky. You're in chains, more chains, a slave now, standing outside a chapel leaking godless audiobooks. You kneel at a shrine where your blood will spill in a complex map—it's a perfect spray, a sacrifice to... what gods? The ones suntanning on bright beach towels.

Spilt gore divides into cells, dismantling the library floor in anomalous patterns of long words etched in poetry yet so full of errors and itchy to your eye. Each close-up is an observation of failure in day-by-day summaries that are shapeless blurs. Normal should be the most obvious thing—it just isn't, divisible like that in an airless space. You're gasping, gasping for air.

"You okay?" Butterfly-on-a-petal eyes against a soft cerulean canvas give you back serenity and you smile at Lily, unsure at first who you are, just overwhelmed by glory. Then you remember it's you. Stu.

And she's white blossom Lily, not gale-eyed Carmille Cabeyo.

You bashfully ask her if she has any books on culture or identity, maybe Morrison, Butler, Shelley, Hopkinson, even Parks. You feel reborn, revolutionised by whatever impossible—that weird-shit eldritch that happened in the library.

As you leave with an essay and a clutch of tomes for yourself, Lily looks at you in a manner that tells you to return the books by their due date, and you will.

You're no more than two steps from the sandstone and quartzite library when the fingers of a blistering draft touch the back of your neck in a way that's focken supernatural. Your clutch of books scatters in a blaze as you tear off running, tripping, falling to make it home let alone Miss Jumanne's class, and it's a longways to split past the corner shop with the comics and reach your suburb without a fancy rod.

The sky ahead steadily changes to a swallowing whirly desert, its storm racing open-mouthed and famished towards you from the horizon. Your feet pound but do nothing because you're not making distance much as you try. You're close to the car park full of gleamers. So you give your all in a sprint—you don't need pumping up.

Maybe you're thinking that surely you can nick and jumpstart a classic, help yourself to some wealth and get the fock away from this shit. Somehow you must reach the car park, and you're super close to the merc or the jag—as in you have choice, and are crash-diving to it—when your strength suddenly fails because the cars have just vanished, and the carpark is empty.

This is the part in a dream where you wake up, but you're fully conscious as the ground begins to fold, sinking you into its foul-smelling gut that's wet and soft like the remains of a dead leprechaun or the regurgitate of a live one. A wave of metallic green hums in real time towards you—it's a plague of flies. You glance backwards, hands clawing for your past, not this torrid, ingesting future and its crawl of maggots wriggly up your ankles. Flies still shooting towards you. Suddenly it's a furnace, everything burning, burning, the critters and pieces of yourself ashing at your feet.

Amid it all there's Carmille Cabeyo standing in shadow at the arched rear window of the school library. Not shaking her head in sadness or frowning her brow in startlement at the wretchedness of you but stretching her lip into what appears to be the start of a smile, eyes scanning with the morbid curiosity one brings to a wake, sweet name of Jesus. Now there's Lily, not-so-delicate Lily, this one is shapeshifting to a Lil-Cabeyo ghoul, and there's nothing honeyed or butterflied about the disquiet you feel.

A wolfing hurricane grants your wish for the past, and it sucks you back to the library, where there's no Lily or Carmille Cabeyo, just arched windows and thick pillars, and you're inside the Harold Holt microfiche room with its painted ceiling. Somehow you can see all this as you howl and quake because your body is in a casket, your neck twisted—you fell off the library ladder, broke your neck. This you know just only now. Yet you're looking at yourself outside in.

On the brink of your betterment, yet too late now in a looping torment.

The lone coffin is near the lip of an entryway that doesn't look safe.

A conveyer belt starts moving, doesn't stop when it ought to, with you banging and hollering inside out.

This is not an illusion, purgatory, or juju. This is hell.

The library lights up with music, a lilted ditty that sounds debatably tribal, chorusing you towards what can only be a cremating end of the world.

Namulongo and the Edge of Darkness

A Lot of Selfless Running

A SEA GHOST grips Namulongo's hand in a place of lost and found. It wisps in and out in fog, its floating mist swallowing her fears. It ebbs and flows, reacquaints itself with shadow and hiss, sound and image in unevenness that's a questioning, and also a learning. But what's not learning is the fog's growth. Each year's swell is disproportionate to its past. What's not learning is the sea ghost's warmth, how it slips in night and day as Namu tosses and turns in her sleep. What it gives is solace in a familiar face of ambivalent light. At the distant edge of her distraction, the fog dances and smoothes her flaws. It stretches her to a wakefulness that's the best for now, guides her into a chapel that has an altar and a grimoire, and then down the basement to a sweeper that's crawling the ocean.

Namulongo's mother knows about her dreams. This is fact, Namu knows. So she doesn't tell her mother everything, especially in the gut of a chore, like now.

"Eee, pampula," exclaims Maé. "What a season you're having, child. I've never seen you guide the sweeper to this big a catch."

"Maybe I was just lucky."

"Luck has nothing to do with it. You've come of age and simply know how to harvest."

"My life feels like a lot of selfless running."

"And that's a selfish thing to say." Maé clicks her tongue.

"I'm just saying—"

"Well, don't."

Namu follows closely, imitates her mother's cleverness with the fish. Maé's hands move swifter with annoyance, her eyes wearing the blackness of a rare pearl, a deep, deeper, deepest ebony. Her eyes gleam silver when she chants before the altar. Maé is a magus of the coven, but she never magics the fish. With Namu by her side, who needs a chant to catch a good harvest from the ocean?

They work tirelessly and isolate the thrashing fish trapped in *Submerse*'s sweepers.

"This one you let go." Maé uses the gentle picker to prong the wolf-fish and its terrible face down the pressure shoot, and back into the black waters.

"I know, Maé."

"You know, because I'm a good teacher."

"Yes, Maé."

At nine cycles, Namu knows a lot about the ocean and its creatures. She knows enough about *Submerse*, her underwater home, and the chores it insists she performs. She bustles from dawn to dusk, bow to stern, running, running in its tight quarters segmented into compartments.

The workshop is one compartment. Here, they make and recycle water, some from the facility that flushes open-valved with a pressured tank. The sleeper is a tiny unit. Here, they take turns in alternating sleep—it's called a warming, where Namu sleeps just off her mother's waking, her warmth on the bed still. It's a shared bunk bed and there's an equally shared locker full of handwoven thermals. The cooker is both a kitchen and a diner. It's next to a hive that has brown bees, all fuzzy-bodied, black-striped. The hive is honeycombed, its honey full of nuts, spice, ocean and smoke.

Near the cooker is a veggie patch. It's more spacious inside than one might expect, and it's reminiscent of something Namu remembers, then forgets. It's as if the growth of each new plant or habitat reinvents the veggie patch, mutates it to optimal conditions. The patch has miniature coconuts that yield sweet and sour water and cream flesh when you crack them. It grows wild lettuce, green tea, chilli pepper, black pepper, baby arrowroot, black nightshade, stinging nettle, shona cabbage, red eggplant, native sunflower, and all. The oxygen chamber has an electrolysis machine that winks green to show the oxygen is right. In the engine room, there's a spare battery and a powered generator that steers *Submerse* through the oceans.

"The moon, the stars—they're our friends," Maé always says.

In the comms room, when the signal is right, Auntie Azikiwe flickers in and out from her enchanted prison. There's a bridge at the top of *Submerse*. The vessel surfaces at dusk, and the watchtower has a periscope for Namu to study the world.

Maé expects much, and Namu gives it. She's good at scrubbing the hulls and the showers and the chambers. She paints to keep *Submerse*'s tough steel from rusting. They don't have a titanium vessel like Aunt Umozi's. The same Umozi who, in her cunning, commandeered Auntie Azikiwe's submersible and all its power, reinforcing her own physical and charmed supremacy. Aunt Umozi wants Maé and Namu dead. She flickers in and out of the comms transmitter display when she breaches the vessel's firewall, or a surface drone catches a roaming signal. Namu has seen enough of the laughing face and its white, white teeth—let alone her mother's jumpiness when they appear. She's heard enough of the displaced sound to know that Umozi is abysmal, and it started with the Fallout.

Maé will not speak of the Fallout. But Auntie Azikiwe, when the drone picks a signal, and if Maé is absent, has hinted of it. It's a Fallout that happened way before Namulongo, and has cascaded to worse. All Namu knows is that she and Maé are outcast, and Auntie Azi is held captive in her own submerse. All of them are in grave danger. From what Namu has gleaned from stolen conversations, Umozi has grown more powerful since the Embodiment, but no-one will explain the details.

"Can't you get back in favour?" Namu once asked Maé.

"That's beyond question."

Today, Namu looks at the sweeper's harvest. She isolates the fish in buckets. She remembers everything Maé taught her, because Namulongo is a curious one. And curiosity is good for learning. She isolates fish by shape and hue. The silver and blue of the baby bluefin. The treble fin of the mud-coloured cod. The untidy splotch of the flounder. The sleek line of the silver bass. The leopard spots of the trout. Today is a very good catch.

Some play dead fish. *Stun those first.* That's what Maé likes to say. *Hold them by the tail, give a solid whack on the head. Or if you know where the brain is, pierce it with a blade tip.* Namu knows where the brain is. Sometimes an auto-stunner does the job. *Put the head in first.* It's humane that way. Because playing dead means being cunning. And that kind of sly means the fish's woe is more. They know if you pour an ice slurry over them, and play deader, until they can't. It's cruel to suffocate fish. To see them gasp for air and convulse. To see them contort their bodies until the thrashing goes weak. *Behead quickly, gut,* says Maé. Or just gut. Vertical along the base, peel the tail back. Pull the guts, bone the fillet. Now the fish is really dead. And fresh. Leave the carcass in the cool reefer, until it dumps the smell of the ocean.

"Go and have a splash," says Maé.

"But I washed this morning."

"Eee, pampula. I've never known a girl to hate water. We have lessons, soon after, no?"

"Yes, but—"

"But nothing. You purify to cast a spell. And, after the lesson, dinner."

Maé doesn't get that it's not the water that Namu dislikes. It's the restraint that comes with it. Drip, drip. Recycled, drip. From an early age, Namu has understood that what she needs is tiny wetness, turn off the faucet. Soap, drip, drip. Dry. Even brushing her teeth is on drip, drip. Wet the brush, turn the water off. Brush to and fro, *remember the tongue.* To and fro, don't forget the cheeks. Spit, turn the water back on. Drip, drip.

Namu is a water creature. It's torment to withhold water for one whose spirit is water. So she avoids the washing in the manner her mother demands, same as she dislikes sleeping. The bunk is a coffin. Her awareness of the tomb that is her home is big, because that very home also drifts through the ocean and its endless flow.

Isolate the Flame from the Wick

Namulongo and her mother kneel by the altar inside a candle-lit chapel.

"I'll teach you to light the flame different," says Maé.

"Why?"

"Your borrowed spell is lacking. Soon, you must whisper your own chant, not mine."

"But I don't have an incantation."

"You'll find it."

"How?"

"Sometimes people dream an 'own' chant. Sometimes you create one."

"I don't need magic language. Maé, I don't want to become a magus."

"You're born to the coven."

"Am I, Maé?"

"Eee, pampula. This sacred place is not for arguing. Fetch me the grimoire."

Namu lifts the magic tablet from its lectern, left to the altar. She hands it to Maé, seated cross-legged on a carpet of cured antelope skin.

"What did I teach you about this text?"

"It's a book of shadows. It has your thoughts, recipes, spells, rituals and hexes—every single one of them personal to you."

"Soon we'll start on your grimoire. Now do as I do."

Maé rolls her eyes and begins to shudder in a chant:

Inasa bwira

Nada ina.

Flames go out in the array of candles. "Light them again."

Namulongo casts her hand, palms out as if to summon, or to channel. She gazes inwards, sways in a chant:

In asa bwi ra

Na da ina.

The flame on the wicks flickers weakly.

"Walk me through it," says Maé. "What are you trying to do when you spell?"

"What you asked. I want to make the spell talk."

"Eee, pampula. That's what is going wrong. You need to *talk the spell*. You must *become* the spell—don't think yourself through it."

"I don't understand, Maé. I never will."

"A spell is about belief. Feel it here." Maé touches Namu's head. "And here." Namu's chest. "And here." Namu's stomach. "Now straighten up and do it right."

In asa bwi ra

Na da ina

"Better. See how the flame is bold? This time I want you to toss it."

"How?"

"Isolate the flame from the wick."

In asa bwi ra

Na da ina

"Say it like you own it. Draw deep, then breathe your intent in a quick release."

In asa bwi ra—

"Child, there's not enough on your breath. Your throat is not even moving. You need to hang onto belief until the spell homes."

"I'm trying, Maé!"

"Try harder. On a battlefield if you leave a spell hanging, enemies will pounce. They read you like their own grimoire."

In asa bwi ra—

"Where's your conviction?"

"I'm doing my best. How can I succeed if you keep intruding?"

"Because it kills me to see you doing it wrong. You have the right 'initiate'. What you need is a good 'finish'."

In asa bwi ra!

Na da ina!

Namu heaves forward and throws her arms. Orange-blue flames surge from the wicks. They shoot to the chapel's tough steel roof, and flutter in a sizzle, dead on their fall.

"Child." Maé lays a hand on Namulongo's shoulder. "The spell has too much carry. You lost your temper."

"Then stop pushing me!"

"Know composure, even in distress. Never let the enemy read your weakness."

"It's hard to find the craft when you don't want it."

"Feel the spell."

"I need time to settle, Maé."

"Composure is all the settle you need."

By the end of the lesson—Maé still pushing her relentlessly into the world of spells—Namu is spent, body and mind.

"The best time to find your core in a spell is when you need it the most," Maé is saying. "Endure the challenge—an attack can happen quickly. Sometimes all you need is to keep the enemy at bay, until help arrives." She ruffles Namu's plaits. "That's the last lesson for today. Accept when you need help. Now, go take a nap."

"You said dinner after. I'm not little anymore—I don't need naps!"

"Even while I surface *Submerse*, then you'll wake for a swim? Trust Bibi, she'll guide you."

The fog of Maé's familiar—the sea ghost—envelops Namu. She finds herself in the bunk bed, her mother's voice a whisper in the distance.

A nap is not a game of statues, just a holding of breath. Sleep, child, in the season of the oceans. Today is upwelling. Seabirds nest and, when you rouse, you can watch whales leaping in the rise and fall of spring winds. I'll make you a flower pickle that protects you from the edge of darkness. Hibiscus petals, sunflower oil, vinegar, thyme and garlic, all sealed in a jar with a spell of origin and conquest. One lick will sigh out the blackness after sundown. Next lick, it'll march you to the horizon, out to see a victory. The battle belongs to you, child. Bloom, bloom, this moonlight, sleep in the ocean's belly.

Maga kasi... Osi osi.

A sea ghost hums this.

Put Up the Drone

Namulongo wakes to a sensation of floating. She remembers drifting to a faraway place.

Then someone calling: "Namulongo." Her head is light.

"Namu! Put up the drone. It's your auntie."

"Maé—"

"The signal is bad. Do it now."

Namu climbs down the bunk, finds her knees and races inside tight walls to the comms room next to the engine room. She dials the special transmitter. The signal on the soundwaves and the microphone look good. She boosts the audio amplifier and presses the button that

155

commands the visual drone out the tower, now on the ocean surface, as *Submerse* goes to rises at the turn of dusk.

Namu joins Maé in a protected control chamber, secured as extra defence from Umozi. She puts on her goggles. There's Auntie Azikiwe, chest up on the screen, bobbing in what looks like space, but it's a compartment inside her submersible where she's imprisoned. The blue-green pearls in her eyes light with recognition. Her hair resembles ferns, the slippery kind that falls to her shoulders. She's yellow-skinned, sinewy-framed.

"Chile, you've come of age, your mother tells me." Her sweet voice in song.

"It's lonely here."

"But you have me, no?" says Maé. "You have no need to worry your aunt with the little things."

"... your own familiar—" Auntie Azikiwe's sound is breaking in and out.

Namu is not strong on magic, but she likes very much the idea of having her own familiar, like Maé and Auntie Azi.

Auntie Azikiwe's familiar is Walli, a whale. She clicks, whistles, pulses and blows air from her nose. A whale that calls—Namu would love that. Or a brook horse that lets her ride its back in foggy weather. Or a water sprite, gap-toothed and woolly-haired, moving between worlds of the living and the dead. No, a dolphin or a whale are enough. But... Namu feels sad. Auntie lost Walli to Umozi. Miniatured into a house pet, a most cruel thing.

"... remind me of myself, so bright—"

Namu agrees that she's bright, and likes it that Auntie Azikiwe sees herself in Namu.

Maé peers at the screen. "Azi, are you well?"

"... don't know my coordinates—"

"We'll find you, my sister."

"... at the edge of darkness—"

"Give us a better clue, Azi. Are you imprisoned in your own submersible still?"

"... can't control it... displacing me with spells... scatters my signal every few—"

"Just hang on tight."

"... don't have long... By the time we're done on this call—"

"Stay sane, dear one."

"... elsewhere—"

"Be careful. Umozi is getting more dangerous daily."

"... give anything to see the world, to see you—"

"You cannot cure spite, but we'll beat Umozi at her game."

"... running out of food, air and water—"

"Keep using what magic you have left." Maé's gaze at Namulongo is full of message. "Namu needs to learn more magic. But we'll reach you."

"We'll find you, Auntie Azikiwe."

"... mother tells me you have an appetite for spells—"

"I want to be a land voyager," says Namu.

"Eee, pampula. You're a child of the water. Why do you wish to abandon it?" reproaches Maé.

"... isten to your moth—" A sound scratch, then a screech. Auntie Azikiwe glares, wobbles in broken signal and Namu hears the remnants of a chant:

... *ozi tasi—*

The screen goes black.

"Azi? Azi!"

"Auntie Azikiwe!"

"Child, you see why I need you to focus on the spells?"

"We'll find her, Maé."

"We must. None of that nonsense about land voyaging."

Stay Hungry for the Ocean

Namu stands on the bridge, faces outwards at the yawn of the horizon. She's surprised it's still light, though it's dusk. *Submerse* is pre-set to rise to the surface at sundown. In the belly of the metal tube of her undersea home, it's impossible to keep time. Looking out at the waters, Namu feels at one with the ocean.

Dark waves nuzzle each other in a playful stretch, now apart, now they belong together. That which binds them is old and new, just like Namu. She looks out to where she yearns to swim across, and wonders where she might go if she leapt. But she's uncomfortable with the thought, unsure if she crossed the light to the edge of darkness... would she ever want to come back?

She understands the seasons of the oceans. In Upswelling, creatures of the water nest, and she can watch the whales. Winterstorm brings turbulence. A winter squall shimmers frosty air on the cool waters, so rough. In Oceanic, the tide is relaxed, at its quietest. The surface gets warm, and the water clear.

A silhouette of birds soars above the ocean.

Namu strips naked from her thermal tights that are ultralight and conserve heat. Her sets are woven in bright colours of summer, rainbow, peach, apple, cherry, blood orange, sunflower, but mostly fruit colours. Unlike her mother's bland colours: grey, navy or black ones. Namu changes sets sparingly, to save the washing. She folds today's papaya-hued ones over a swivel chair inside the tower, pitches forward and torpedoes. She loves the feel of the black water on her skin. It's water that goes and goes across all reaches. She catches it in her palms, releases and lets it flow between her fingers. She streamlines on a float, then flutter kicks, kick... her body swivelling away, away... from *Submerse*.

She listens to the short calls of a storm-petrel. It whines like a seal pup.

Namulee, Namulee... she hears the sea ghost's gentle call.

Bibi is translucent, both male and female. Sie can melt in the sun, puddles into water. Sie's a fog when it's cooler. Namulongo turns, reluctant. She faces the vessel that is her home... is it also her prison? No, it's nothing like Auntie Azikiwe's fate. She pitches upwards, a dolphin on water, explosive from the hips through the feet. She splashes again and again, then sculls vertical, treading water.

Namulee, Namulee...

Sometimes when the water is clearer, a pale blue, the light of luminescent creatures matches the moon's. Tonight, she feels the brush of something past her toes, that's all. She can't see below the surface, but knows how deep the waters go.

Namulee, Namulee...

Namulongo floats on her back in a one-arm swim. She feels the gentle swell of waves on the flat waters.

Bibi's fog warms Namu as she pulls on the handwoven thermals, and steps back inside the hatch to lost time. She finds Maé in the cooker. She's adding shrimp in a layer on a pan, removing them as they turn pink, start to curl. She drizzles sunflower oil, salt, pepper. Pulls from the baker a pregnant loaf.

"It smells like I'll be eating *delicious*," says Namu.

"No thanks to me," says Maé. "You and the sweeper, and the flour."

"I didn't do much."

"You roasted the sunflower seeds just right, ground them like someone's paying. Child, why don't you sit? Have a little cassava wine." Maé passes the calabash, breaks the bread. "To the richness of the ocean."

"And the strength of belief," responds Namulongo.

They eat in silence. Namu wonders at the shimmer in the black pearls of Maé eyes. "The water was calm?"

"You know it was calm, Maé. I don't know if it's me or you, or Bibi. The water is always calm."

Maé's studious gaze, then: "Your hunger for it... Child, you'll always stay hungry for the ocean."

"I want to voyage the land."

"If the gods wanted us to be land folk, we'd have been land folk."

"Sometimes we make our own fate, Maé."

"Action, not words, no?"

"In magic, words have power—you said so, Maé. No?"

"You know it's unessential to speak. Silence, especially now, can be bliss."

Dinner is no civil war, but missiles keep coming across their fundamental differences. At the point of death, if it's the point of death, all they'll remember is wine—not the vinegar kind. They'll pick their way across seasons that hum tender and sing fresh. They'll step into reach and find truth. They'll forget the semantics of filial war. Rebirth is reconstituting oneself. It's slipping from a speckled sun and treading in semitone above the minor 5th to a blush moon. Rebirth is whistling bridges that gather reflections and walk their true selves between petty distinctions and cross-lined gaps.

A sea ghost ponders this.

The Fallout

A scratch on the comms room, then a crackle.

Crackle, crackle. "Namulongo. Namu!"

Namu and her mother leap in a stampede. They fall into the soundproofed control chamber. The audio is crisp. Auntie Azikiwe bobs in space sharper than they've seen her. The jungle in her fern hair is wild. The pearls in her eyes are a richer colour of the ocean vacillating between blue and green.

She speaks urgently to Maé. "It's cycles now. Namu is grown, maybe—" song of wind and dawn in her voice.

"She's still a child, Azi."

"I'm not as powerful as before. Fighting Umozi's spells has weakened me. Keeping alive is weakening."

"We're doing our best, Azi."

"I feel trapped in a winter storm, yet I'm inside somewhere."

"You must be far, because here it's a quiet night."

Namu hears a terrible scream, as if someone is strangling a dragon.

"Azi!"

"Auntie Azikiwe!"

Her eyes are panicked. "I must go! Umozi is using me as bait to find you!"

"Take care!"

"... cast a homing spell—" a wavering sound yet delicate as a reed in her voice.

"Don't do anything that will enrage her even more."

"... too late—"

The screen zooms onto Auntie Azikiwe's swollen belly.

"Eee, pampula, Azi! What have you done? Why?"

"... life is miserable as it is... worst that could happen?"

"Umozi, that's what! She's the worst that could happen."

"... necessary—"

"You should only use the spell of creation at your hour of death. To keep the quadity. That's how it's always been. The spell of creation is forbidden!"

"... never stopped you—"

Maé turns her head towards Namulongo—who suddenly comprehends.

"Eee, pampula. See what you've done."

"—about time she knew... my back hurts... hungry all the time, crave soft stone—"

Namu hears a scratch, then a screech.

"Azi!"

"She's coming!"

"—if she knows... communicating... she'll move me another place—"

"Auntie Azikiwe!"

The vision goes black.

Maé removes her goggles at the same time as Namu lifts hers.

They look at each other a long time. There's sadness in Maé's gaze, and Namu feels rage in hers. She's breathing hard.

"Your auntie loves you. She didn't mean to upset you."

"She?"

"Child—"

Namu leaps back, as if Maé's touch might burn. "Am I the Fallout?"

"I can expl—"

"I don't want to hear it from you." Namu can't break the tremor in her voice. "I never want to hear it from you!"

An unborn child folds into the powers of the moon and patterns into raindrops. She's formed by belief. Her palm clasps life in an art of fiction, charts and fortune.

A mother wraps a shawl over her belly, plants a fingertip kiss on her bub.

A sea ghost sees this.

Namu distracts herself with chores as her mother sleeps. She climbs to the tower, steps out of the hatch. A cormorant grunts as it takes off from the metal surface. Oink, oink! It circles the air and grunts as it lands back on *Submerse*. Oink, oink! It stalks, and is large this near, a glossy black, sheeny white. It cocks its head, glares at Namu with its green eye circled orange in a patch on its face, then loses interest. It wobbles its bare throat, opens its grey hooked bill and regurgitates fish.

Namu cuts loose the drone in an action that will offset Aunt Umozi's tracker.

In asa bwi ra!

Na da ina!

The drone erupts in flames on the water, burns itself out, as the cormorant grunts its disdain in flight.

Inside the hatch, Namu wipes down and adjusts the periscope in the looking tower. She closes the hatch, steps back into the windowless *Submerse*. In the engine room, she checks buoyancy, resets the radar and listens for echoes off the seabed.

Once, she caught the signal of a human submarine 10 days away. She steered from it, rewrote the satellite feeds on her itinerant world disconnected from humanity.

Gently, she sinks the vessel, glides in the direction of the next guess at a rescue mission.

The Ocean Stays Hungry

They avoid each other. But inside such close quarters bumping is inevitable when practising rotating sleep. Namu prefers hiding near the pressure hull—the metal that keeps water out. The layout is just so, there's almost a cubicle they sometimes use as storage. The inner hull is resistant to pressure, the outer hull waterproofed.

But Namu can't hide forever in her thoughts. Chores, she needs chores. The shower and its recycled water, drip, drip, three blinks, drip, drip, is in spick condition. In the engine room everything is running fine: fins, diving planes, hydroplanes, propellers that push it forwards, the swivelling flaps for tilt, climb, sink or float.

Her smile is wry. She's been too efficient in her chores. There's not much with which to distract herself in her little city under water. Still, she checks the oxygen chamber—it's lit green and the electrolysis machine is farming good air for *Submerse*. She scrubs inexistent grease and amine from the floors and walls. She visually inspects the hull and mixes plant dye. She scrapes peels onto a drop cloth and uses a putty knife to even the surface. She spreads paint with a roller to prevent rust. She checks the compact machine, ejects trash from the watertight exit in the hull.

She can't help it, but water is calming. She's up on the tower, level with water. She puts her fingers in the warm black water and wants to weep. If she looks too closely her life is neither a bell nor a shell. Nor is it a song. It's been like this since the metaphor of her birth. One step, two steps, she knows a spell, not a prayer. She knows how to get naked. She bends down and forward from the hips, slips rather than throws herself into the ocean.

She tilts herself to float on her back, her head close to flat on the water. She pushes back with her arm, completes a stroke. Kick, kick, flutter kick, as painful thoughts of her parentage roost home. Maé made her using a spell of creation.

Today, it's too deep for snorkelling. When she can, she finds little treasures she likes to think are gifts Auntie Azi has placed for her to find on the seabed: pearls, shells, sea amulets, coral gems... Namu is a collector, both with her hands and eyes. She stores in her memory what she sees: the muddy sheen of the halibut as it glides by. The fluorescent peach of the rock fish. The silver and yellow of the yellowtail—hence its name; it dances away when she makes as if to catch it by its wide tail. The ugly yawn of the grey lingcod.

She wonders if her familiar, when she gets one, might be a wary one—like the pygmy seahorse. It might be a radiant one—like the cherubfish and the tropical blue on its sunflower nose. It could be a shy one. She'll nudge it out from shyness with her fingers if it were a yellowhead jawfish burrowed in sand, shells or rock. She wouldn't mind a pipehorse—shaped between a seahorse and a pipefish. She's not sure about a tiny eel—worming, burrowing in soft sand, swaying in currents. Never the frogfish—all the bumps on its skin, but she might learn to love it. She doesn't really have to love a familiar, just to respect it in a symbiotic partnership. At most, she'll feed it plankton.

As she kicks back to the tower, something playful swims in and out of her vision. At first she thinks it's a baby dolphin. She doesn't mind a dolphin for a familiar—she'll call it Dolpho. She'll watch how it moves fast in the water, blowing bubbles and all chatty. This one is chatty. It's white and black. It nudges her stomach from below, as if pushing her to the surface. It whistles, clicks, squawks. She wonders what it's saying.

She climbs out of the water. It moans, barks, groans and yelps. Looking down from the tower she realises it's not white and black, and certainly not a dolphin. She could have sworn it's the biggest tilapia she has ever seen, but fish don't whistle or click, bark or groan, get all playful in the water. How can her familiar be a tilapia? What would she even call it! Pia? Tipa? Seeing how it nudged her with its bottlenose to the surface, maybe the fish might help her if she were sick or injured. And she'll certainly know the plankton or small fish—headfirst—to feed it. With those rows of baby teeth, it's a wonder it didn't bite her.

It's anyone's guess but Maé says it's time Namulongo got her own familiar.

A blackheaded gull screams out yonder. Namu wonders if perhaps she's got it wrong, and her familiar is a bird. She watches as the fish swims away, farther, farther into the endless blackness of humping waves.

The water is unfinished.

A shadowy moon in the horizon casts a silhouette on the glistening ocean. It begins to rain. Fat drops from the sky fall down, down, and the giant water gobbles each wet pearl, only to reform around itself. No matter what or how much falls into it, *drip*, *splashity* or *splash!* the ocean stays hungry. Like Namulongo. Restless and open to the sky.

Unfinished.

Spell Like It's Survival

"Look at this," says Maé.

Namulongo takes the brand new book and its cover of tempered bark from her mother. She opens it and gasps. "It's unwritten."

"It's yours."

"My grimoire?"

"Your very own. And this." It's a quill pen. "But you must make your own ink."

"How?"

164

"I'll show you. If you can make plant dye, then you can make ink. You can write in whatever colour you want to write your instructions and divinations. A grimoire doesn't grow in a day."

Maé's eyes gleam silver:

Inasa bwira

Nada ina.

"There. No-one can write in it, only you. And look here." Maé runs her fingers along a second lectern, also brand new, next to her own on the altar. "It's a placement for your grimoire."

"I'm good with hands. I could have carved it myself."

"Eee, pampula. This sacred place is not for ungratefulness."

Namu bows her head. "I'm sorry, it's just a little—"

"Overwhelming?"

"Yes."

"Come and sit with me."

They are cross-legged on the carpet of antelope skin. Maé lifts a tiny calabash. She swirls a red liquid that smells like the innards of a rotting wolf-fish. She dips two fingers, and lines the corner of Namu's eyes to her cheekbones.

"I don't like how it smells."

"I'm not asking you to eat it."

"Maé! Will you ask me to?"

"No. It's a ritual bath—today's lesson is a special one. Light the candles."

Namu gazes inwards, sways in a chant:

In asa bwi ra

Na da ina.

"Mhhh."

"Did I not incant well?"

"You can do better."

"But the flame is bold. Look. Do you want me to isolate it from the wick?"

"I did not ask you to do more than light the candles."

"I'm no good. I'll never be as good as you."

"You'll be, when it's right. Your spell memory is good. You just need better instinct."

"All I can be is a spare."

"Even a fish makes a difference. This sacred place is not for self-pity." Maé's gaze is sharp. "Are those tears? Stop this rubbish."

Namu wipes her cheeks with the back of her hand.

Maé touches her lightly on the shoulder. "What you bring to the altar is crucial. Cultivate the eyes of your magic."

"I don't know what you mean..."

"Remember what I said. A spell is about belief. Feel it here," on Namu's head, "and here," Namu's chest, "and here," Namu's stomach. "Today we're doing the spell of battle. When an attack happens, there's no time for self-pity. Do you hear me?"

Namu nods, a lump in her throat still.

"Good. To tell you the truth, I think you're gifted with fire. You're a child of water, but might surprise us with something more. It might be that your familiar will be a dragon."

"A water dragon?"

"A fire one." She studies Namulongo for a while in silence, then says: "Now. I want us to go over the main things you've learnt about spells."

Namu clears her throat. "There are—"

"Louder."

"There are seven main spells. The spell of elements—with it, you command fire, water, air, metal and earth."

"Good."

"The spell of displacement—this one summons imprisonment, like what Aunt Umozi has done to Auntie Azi."

"An unfortunate thing that we are working to make right."

"The spell of embodiment—it allows you to become the other. This spell can also be a spell of heralding, or a homing. A powerful magus can use it to send help or an assassin."

"I'll practice embodiment with you today, after you tell me the remaining spells."

"The spell of growth works on life that already exists. You use it to manipulate plants, hair, nails, small animals and the like. The spell of battle helps you disperse, deter, injure, paralyse, misdirect or intercept the foe. You can summon paralymus to temporarily inhibit a foe so they can't move closer or do you harm."

"Child, you are a sponge. Your theory is astounding. We just need you to get practical."

"The spell of destruction allows you to destroy, burn and disintegrate."

"You must never ever summon this spell unless your life depends on it."

"The spell of creation is forbidden. You use it when you've mastered all the other spells and there's obligation to bring life from nonlife."

Maé avoids Namu's gaze. "Good," she says, too spritely. And then, all serious: "What do you know about a bichwa?"

"It's a water demon with long fingers that drag you deep into the water."

In a blink Maé wisps into nothing, and then billows. A multiplicity of eyes gleam from the dark mist. A beast leaps out of the haze and backhands Namu across the face. The ferocity of the swipe strikes Namu headfirst against the far wall. She begins an incantation as the beast charges towards her through the chapel. It knocks down Namu's spell with a counter and lunges, claws drawn. Namu gazes inwards, throws her palms forward in a chant:

In asa bwi ra!

Na da ina!

The bichwa falls mid-flight to the ground, and shapeshifts back to Maé.

"That was a good intercept," she says.

"What was *that*?"

"To see is to know."

"I don't need *you* to embody a bichwa!"

"You show good commitment. I like it that you now understand the spell of embodiment."

"How is that a lesson?"

"When an attack happens, you won't always have time or space to respond. Sometimes you're lucky if you get a look, that's all."

"I could have decimated you, Maé!"

"You need extra reach for that. Child, you haven't mastered it."

"Is that blood from your eye?"

"It's nothing. You look like you're in trouble—you haven't moved."

"Aawww."

"Is it ribs that you're clutching?" Maé offers a hand. "Here, let me—"

"Aawww."

"It's just a bruise, nothing serious. But you'll be sore."

"Aawww."

"Take a few minutes. You need a breather."

"What I need is my mother to stop attacking me."

"It's just a bichwa."

"A big one."

"That's a baby one."

"It's still big."

"It matters not."

"To me, it does. The opponent is too much."

"Doesn't look it. Only a fool expects a similar-sized opponent. Clean up the mess and find me in the cooker." Maé turns at the doorway. "Just so you know—that spell was just flicking a finger. In a real battle, all you do with a flick like that is agitate them."

"I did nothing wrong!"

"It's a scrapping start, but you'll get it. Spell like it's survival. Our lives could depend on it."

Namu feels undone. She's at a loss about whether to bellow or curse.

Maé, still at the door, is unfinished. "I can smell you from here. I've never known a girl to dislike water. You're too salty. At least take off those thermals."

To See the End, Look at the Beginning

Namulongo tends the veggie patch to compose herself before preparing a meal. The sunflowers are doing well. They yield strong-flavoured seeds that make good oil. She uses a cold press to remove the hulls, breaks the seeds into smaller pieces and runs them through the warm press of a steel roller to squeeze out the oil. She enjoys the aroma of roasting seeds in a pan, stirring them frequently. She then grinds them into a fine meal texture and lets the blend cool. She pours it through a strainer, and sieves out the oil.

Maé has also taught her to make plain flour. Namu's thinking this as she digs out an arrowroot for dinner, snaps some black nightshade leaves and shoots. She plucks some nettle. Sometimes she wonders if Maé likes her at all. Namu is not sure what's the distinction between tough love and soundless hate. But Maé's love or hate is filled with sound. She wraps her barbs with adages:

"To see the end, look at the beginning."

"Be lost to know the way."

Now she sits unperturbed, full-lipped, with her tight black hair and smooth sheen on her skin, as if nothing happened. She's knitting new thermals with special needles. The rich melon hue suggests the thermals are for Namulongo.

Namu is good at cooking with limited produce. She peels, washes and steams the arrowroot. She blanches the nightshade and stir-fries the stinging nettle to add taste. It goes best with turnips but also works with arrowroot. Sometimes she uses it in a soup, and Maé can make nettle beer.

Namu fillets a fish vertical along the base, peels the tail back and bones it. She adds it to the steamer, takes it out before Maé can say, "You're overcooking it."

Maé prefers live crab or lobster, boiled alive. Looks and tastes better that way. The shock of a scalding makes the legs fall off. Kills bacteria too, no food poisoning. All she needs is a pan of salted water, heated not too long. The crab or lobster is already dead in a few blinks. Leave to cool. There are no consequences for dinner.

"To the richness of the ocean," says Maé.

"And the strength of belief," responds Namu.

For how long? Namu imagines herself on land, all the wind racing in laughter behind her as they run.

She wants to voice this to her mother, but instead says, "Do you want extra pickle?"

"The octopus one."

"Okay."

First, Ask Me a Riddle

Up on the tower, the air shimmers. There's no sight of land all around, just waves and waves of the ocean.

Sheesheeshaashaa.

At first, Namu is not sure she's heard it right. But the whispers rise again from the water.

Sheesheeshaashaa.

And then she hears a distressed cry, *Namulee, Namulee...* the sea ghost.

Bibi in hir fog is immobile at the hatch, unable to seep out. Namulongo knows without asking about the paralymus spell. It's a spell of battle. She looks around for Aunt Umozi, or her assassin.

Sheesheeshaashaa.

It's then that Namu sees the nymph. It slips from the water's churn. The creature is a knot of guts and twine that roams in shape until it morphs into a blue-skinned beast of many heads and tails. Its nose is flat, its mouth lipped. Its cheeks are as plump as a newborn's. It arrows a missile of crabs and starfish in the colours of blood. The gore inks with the nymph's vomit in a rainbow. The ocean humps and the black skies swirl in a tall tale, legend or dream that's just too real for Namu.

Maé warned her she might encounter a nymph in an underwater cave. She told her how one may appear as a fluorescent male. How it can conjure storms and wear many faces that lure the young into the water.

Sheesheeshaashaa.

"See something you like?"

You, you, dear child, child...

"Mustn't you first ask me a riddle?"

The blue nymph rises on tentacles above water. *What is light as fog, fog, but you cannot hold it for long, long?*

"If I solve your riddle, will you leave me alone?"

Of course, course...

"Have I reassurance to trust your word?

The nymph laughs. *No, no...*

Namulongo thinks of Bibi, the sea ghost, but has anyone tried to hold sie for long?

What is light as fog, fog—

"I think it's a spell," says Namu.

Wrong, wrong. Try again, again...

"How about one's breath?"

True, but it won't count, count...

"You said I could trust you!"

If you solved, solved, in one go, go...

"Then ask me another riddle."

What's in a cave, cave and has one hundred eyes, eyes yet cannot see?

"But I am of the ocean. How would I know what lies in a cave?"

What, what...

"I think it's a honeycomb?"

What house is dark, dark, it has not lights, lights...?

"But I already answered your riddle."

Time waste, waste... what, what... is dark, dark...

"The ocean's belly."

Wrong, wrong. Try again, again...

"A tomb."

True, but it won't count, count... Sheesheeshaashaa... so hungry...

Namu gazes inwards, locks her fist, and wills a spell.

In asa bwi ra!

Na da ina!

I command you to leave me!

The blue nymph laughs.

Maybe, maybe, try again, again...

Namu summons her belief.

In asa bwi ra!

Na da ina!

I said leave me!

The blue nymph laughs as its tentacles climb from the water and onto the tower.

Fail a simple, task, task, to finish a riddle, riddle... Now a spell, spell? Your blood so tasty, tasty... pull you under...

Namulee, Namulee... Bibi's distressed call from the hatch, but sie cannot move from the paralymus spell.

Ma ga ka si

Osi osi.

The nymph falls back, briefly stunned.

"Stay down!"

Then it rises on tentacles and bursts in speed on the water surface.

Ma ga ka si

Osi osi.

Namu swirls the spell in her palms, and hurls it.

The nymph ducks the awkward spin of Namu's spell that sizzles dead. The nymph deflects the next spell as it bounces several times in its attack. A splash of tentacles on water smothers the next spell, and the ocean gets the brunt of it. The nymph is now skittling onto the tower.

Maga kasi

Osi osi.

Namu runs and jumps near the edge, and releases her spell. The nymph battles in a clash of wills, and Namu is losing. Out of the corner of her eye she sees a kapu—monkey-like with its moon head, rising from the waves. She feels outnumbered.

"You're within range," she hears Maé, but moves close, closer, until she's directly in front of the nymph along *Submerse*'s edge.

"Hold it," cries Maé. "Hold the spell! Create a path and build. Hold it, now drag it back and release!"

"I said, stay down!" The spell of destruction disintegrates the nymph while an arrow of flame chars the kapu's pipe nose and yellow-green scales. It roars a giant cry and charges in a flourish of anger or hunger.

Maga kasi

Osi osi.

Namu's spell fills the kapu's moon head with water, and ruptures it with a ferocious pop that stains the waves yellow-green. The creature drowns.

"That's. An. Overcommit," says Maé.

"One must never summon the spell of destruction unless life depends on it," says Namu. "It depended." Her voice is flat. She doesn't know what to feel. What she knows is that she's not in the mood to argue with her mother.

"An attack can happen quickly," says Maé gently. "Then instinct is what's left." She looks at Namu. "And those beasts will stay down."

"Quiet night, hey?"

"You showed me up today." She studies Namu with pride. "I could do with more practice."

"Did I sustain the challenge?"

"More than, child. And what was that 'own incantation' that I heard?"

"I dreamt my spell."

"Eee, pampula. That is wonderful to hear. What is left for you is to get your own familiar."

"I saw one in the water."

"I always thought it would be a dolphin."

"It wasn't a dolphin"

"What then? A whale?"

"Tilapia."

"A what?"

"So I guess I can't eat fish if my familiar is a tilapia."

"Just like that?"

"I've always wondered about the sweeper. I'm not sure I like it."

"That's the most 'complete' I've ever heard you in words and seen you action, child. You're a short one, but don't you have the leap!"

"I thought you'd reproach me about the sweeper, or not wanting to eat fish, Maé."

"Why in goddess Samaki's name would I do that?"

Too Much Doom

Maé smiles at the hue of Namulongo's papaya thermals. "Bright like that, no wonder beasts find you."

"Maybe they smell me first."

Their laughter is together.

"Is Bibi going to be alright, Maé?"

"I think so. Sie's a bit sore."

"Oh."

"More hir ego. Sie's more embarrassed than wounded or disappointed about the paralymus spell."

"About being unable to save me?"

"Not like you need saving."

"The attack means that Aunt Umozi knows where we are. She'll send more assassins."

"Her spell of embodiment is clearly more powerful than my woeful demonstration of a bichwa."

"Shall we wait and fight? I am capable now."

"That you are, child." Maé smiles. "But we must drift elsewhere, away from here. It's foolish to wait for more assassins."

Namu commands the engine and steers *Submerse* into a new direction, one that might hopefully converge with Auntie Azikiwe's prison. Right now, everything is going on chance.

"I miss her." Namu says. She's seated on the ground between her mother's feet.

"I know," says Maé, not asking who. Her fingers pull, tug and weave Namulongo's hair into new plaits.

"Aunt Umozi is too much doom."

"That she is."

A scratching sound in the comms room, then a crackle. Crackle, crackle.

Namu leaps at the same time as her mother.

"Azi!"

"Auntie Azikiwe!"

They snatch the goggles and put them on to a blast of distorted music. A laughing face flickering in and out of the screen. Crimson lips, rows and rows of teeth.

"Got yourself into a pickle." Barking laughter.

"Umozi," spits Maé. "I should have known you'd try to boast. Yet you're hiding behind a mask, too scared to show your true self."

The music rubs and grinds. It cascades into more dissonant laughter. "What if the mask is me, too powerful for you now."

"I'd say you're a bit heavy-footed, and need to get quicker with that spell of embodiment. See how quickly we dispatched your friends."

"It was a small fumble, is all. Next time, it's serious business. I'll not toy with you."

"Eee, pampula. When we catch you, we'll see who's toying."

Aunt Umozi's laughter is more wrong than ever. It's the terrible scream of a burning crowd. "Azikiwe is now my pet."

"Where is she?"

"I moved her to where you'll never find her. You thought you could communicate with her in secret. Well, you bit off a lot to chew. What you need is a solid gut. Because you have nowhere to grow your power."

"That's where you're wrong."

"Of course. Your creation."

"She is my daughter! And she strengthens the quadity!"

The laughter wrapped in high-pitched shrieking is unbearable. A piercing brightness on the screen fills Namu with sounds that yank from her core an internal monologue that is a folding and an absence. It's the sigh of a forgotten sun. It's the reek of a seeping wound. It's the underfoot crunch of a live snail's shell. It's the finger-crush of a squirming worm.

Each sound gets bigger and worse, distinct yet united in its disjointedness. The warm wetness of a wren's tears. The uncomely writhe of a beheaded snake. The crimson sprout of a kudu's vein. The neat doubling of a bub in the tentacles of a receding squid. The century-old rot of a wolf-fish. The pale mushiness of a stillborn whale. The dreadful gust of a daemon's breath. The dulling flicker in the eyes of a dying magus.

Namu snatches off the goggles, at the same time as Maé. They fall into each other's arms in comfort. "That will never sound right at all. Never," says Namu against her mother's chest.

"Child. I have no words for what we've just witnessed."

"In magic, words have power—you said it, Maé."

"My spell doesn't have the journey to do what I want with Umozi."

"I have belief."

"Yes. Now you need *real* belief.

"I've got it."

"It's chained until you know the truth of what happened."

"Then tell me."

"I don't know how to."

"Then you could undo the Fallout."

"Child, you know I cannot put you back."

"Maybe you can."

Maé's grip on Namulongo's shoulder hurts. "Do you understand, *really understand*, what you're asking of me?"

Their eyes are at war. Namu blinks first.

"I guess I need to hear the truth."

"Namulongo, you are more than you know."

"Tell me, Maé, how I am more."

"Will you hear it from Bibi, my child?"

All Things Are Never Equal

A sea ghost grips Namulongo's hand in a place of lost and found, and this time there's a dream. The fog wisps in and out of a tale, ebbing and flowing, reacquainting itself with shadow and hiss. The sound and image are an unevenness that's also a myth.

Gods are always fighting to determine dominion over others, but this was something else.

The story goes that Samaki, the goddess of water, knew that her powers were growing. She was tired of living in the heavens, worn with the fighting, eternally on guard. Her three brothers, Tamoi, Pose and Daga, were flawed. They behaved irrationally, and were always jealous of her strength, though they were more beautiful. Even while Samaki came out strong each battle, she suspected her brothers were uniting in a plot against her.

When Tamoi tried to assault Samaki, and put her in a weakened state, that was the last straw. He had mellowed her with wine, crept into her chamber as she slept, but she'd woken. Enraged, she took away his beauty.

Tamoi despised his scales and horned nostrils, and now conspired even harder with his brothers Pose and Daga to destroy Samaki. In last resort, Samaki fled from the skies and into waters, where she chose to personify herself as a magus. Her brothers sent assassins, but a goddess as powerful as Samaki was not an easy target to track or kill. They were getting closer, so to mask her trace even more, Samaki split herself into a quadity of magi and sent each on their way. She

176

appointed the first magus as a priestess of rivers and lakes, the second as a priestess of oceans and seas, the third as a priestess of water creatures, and the fourth a priestess of seabeds and islands.

Each magus mastered seven spells:

The spell of elements: fire, water, air, metal, earth

The spell of displacement

The spell of embodiment

The spell of growth

The spell of battle

The spell of destruction

The spell of creation

This last spell, the spell of creation, was genesis. It was one a magus summoned at her hour of death, to ensure continuity. Calling up the spell created a new magus, who came out fully formed. Things stayed this way across generations, a child magus replacing each of the quadity at their dying, and the quad was always four.

The time came, and the coven of magi begot Umozi, a priestess of rivers and lakes; Maé, a priestess of oceans and seas; Tatu, a priestess of water creatures; and Azikiwe, a priestess of seabeds and islands.

A quadity is perfect, but all things are never equal. There's always a hierarchy. When magi are given to silence, disrespecting the power of dialogue, a challenge will smear its face across amity. Umozi felt short-changed with her rivers and lakes. She wanted the oceans and seas that were bigger. She craved dominion over water creatures, and also coveted the treasures from islands and seabeds.

Fearing the other three magi might grow stronger, Umozi lured Tatu, the most trusting one, to a summit that culminated in a spell of destruction. Umozi overcame Tatu, consumed her powers and her vessel. The killing and swallowing made Umozi exceedingly powerful. But the quadity was broken—three priestesses remained, one a duality.

A quad is balance. Killing Tatu was imbalance.

Fearing challenge—greed and malice guiding her choices—Umozi knew she could never survive the ordeal of embodying a third priestess: Azikiwe. So she imprisoned Azikiwe. Because Maé's powers to command the seas and the oceans were growing, and her capacity to consume Azikiwe was possible—it didn't matter that Maé intended no such a thing. By imprisoning Azikiwe, Umozi knew that Maé could never create her own duality stronger than Umozi's.

The imbalance brought upon the world floods, drought, earthquakes, bushfires, hurricanes, pandemics... And so Maé devised a solution in a spell of creation that summoned a new magus to become the fourth priestess in a quadity that restored harmony. But the new magus was a child, unlearned.

Because Maé had invoked the spell before its time.

A sea ghost tells this.

A Tornado of Flames

The bunk is still warm from Namu's sleep when Maé enters. "It's time for my rotation."

"The idea of sleep has never made you look this happy before, Maé."

"You're always so perceptive, child."

"Those are evasion words, the kind I'd expect from someone who means to tell me nothing."

Maé ruffles Namu's head, snatches her in a quick hug-and-release. "I am happy. Let that be enough."

Namu has an uncanny feel of things. It doesn't always happen, but tonight she has an urgent need to go to the tower. She indulges Maé's carefree mood, as if a burden has been lifted.

"Make me wine while I sleep," says Maé. "I soaked up some maize last night."

Namulongo puts the maize in a pestle. She uses a mortar to pound it. She puts the crushed maize in a large clay pot. She plucks four lemons from the veggie patch and squeezes the juice. She slices the rind to thin, adds it and the lemon juice to the crush in the pot. She puts in boiling water, adds sugarcane syrup, a scoop of old wine and its ferment, and tightens the lid on the clay pot. The new wine will sit for a week, then be ready for drinking.

But there's more wine on the racks for when Maé wakes.

"That was a nap," protests Namu. "You can sleep more, you know."

"I want to see how the ferment went."

"And you'll see nothing!" Namu slaps her mother from the lifting the clay pot's lid. "The wine is brand new." She hands Maé a calabash. "Here, I poured you some from the stock."

"Did you taste it?"

"I am a child."

Maé laughs. "Eee, pampula, these games we play. I didn't hear you bringing up childhood when I offered you cassava wine."

"I like the cassava one better."

"What you need is the right ingredient, and you'll like them all. You won't care if it's maize, cassava or sorghum wine."

Up at the tower in the still night, Namu is contemplative.

The big tilapia is out there, circling *Submerse*. It's chittering and beckoning, as if to reassure of its friendliness. Then suddenly it cries and dives below the surface. An albatross glides long and high, riding the ocean wind without a single flap of its giant wings. It makes a sweeping turn, swoops into the waters and soars to the skies with a fish.

Namu looks at the ocean, and appreciates its beauty. And, right now, she *feels* more than sees. What she feels is warmth towards Maé. Now that Namu understands her family story more, she's become sentimental about Maé's teaching. And Maé is always teaching, even when she's remonstrating:

To see the end, look at the beginning.

Cultivate the eyes of your magic.

You cannot cure spite.

To see is to know.

Even a fish makes a difference.

Be lost to know the way.

An attack can happen quickly...

It all makes sense to Namu now. What doesn't make sense is the ball of flame now falling from the sky. Entranced, Namu studies the fire whirl, and falls back when the tornado of flames the colour of the sun shimmers in a trail and crashes into the waves.

Namu curses Aunt Umozi, and steadies herself for the spell of battle.

In her mind's eye, as she waits in the terrible silence, she sees all brutes of monsters: a giant squid that would drown the vessel; a malevolent water sprite with bad spirits from the dead; a pregnant gorgon with the hair of venomous snakes; an ancient bichwa with nothing to lose.

She gazes inwards, sways in the beginning of a chant—

Namulee, Namulee... the sea ghost floats and hovers on the ocean between Namulongo and the grey thing bobbing on the surface.

Kraa, kra, it cries weakly.

It sounds like a newborn—not that Namu has seen many, she did see a seal pup once—

Kraa, kra.

Namu drops her pose of attack readiness. She leaps into the waters and the sea ghost lets her reach the crying thing. Kraa, kra. Namu floats back with her rescue, and the tilapia is helping. It nudges them on board with its bottlenose.

The charred bird falls on Namu's wet lap, her thermals sodden.

Namulee, Namulee... the sea ghost floats and wraps Namu and the bird in hir fog. Hir heat gently dries Namulongo and the bird that's not a bird, she's now sure. It squeaks weakly, tired, and has feathers now fluffed up on crooked wings. But its face—

Kraa, kra.

"I guess you're sore," says Namu. "And hungry."

Bibi's fog floats them to the cooker, and finally Namu can be astonished. Maé looks up from the diner, where she's seated.

"I don't get it, Maé. Bibi is always so protective, of *me*. Sie practically raised me from your meanness."

"And now sie's protecting this one." Maé studies the bird that's not a bird, its wing at an angle.

"Protecting? Fawning!"

Maé tries to touch it but it nips at her. "Look at its face. I think it's a baby phoenix."

"*How* can it be?" Namu studies the ugly thing that's all crooked and depressed, plucking its feathers, crying weakly and refusing to eat.

"Look at its dropping."

"Yes, only one."

Maé picks the dropping, rubs it on the veggie patch soil until it sparkles. "I'd say this is amethyst."

"So a ball of flame falls from the sky, it wails like a baby, poops gemstones—and you say it's a phoenix?"

"My best guess," says Maé. "Call it a she, and Bibi loves her."

"Let's call her Phoena."

Shackery-in-a-Cabin

Phoena's recovery is swift. She fluffs her feathers on Namu's face with glee, her wing less angled. She has a penchant for sunflower seeds, nightshade shoots, the tiny white flowers of the shona cabbage, shrimp, and sorghum wine. She steals pecks of wine from Maé's calabash and, having mastered the lid, can push it aside and sully new ferments with a mouth in.

"Let's throw the darn thing back where it came from."

"Auntie Azikiwe said she cast a homing spell. Perhaps Phoena is it?"

"Maybe you have a point. But she's so annoying."

"Don't you wonder how come Bibi is so adoring and protective of her?"

"Still annoying. And it takes some getting used to her face. She reminds me of you as a baby."

"Ugly?"

"No, child. What I mean is that Phoena has a baby face."

"Maé! The hatch won't open!"

"Don't be lazy. Just push."

It's an obstruction nobody wants.

"Really, it won't! I've turned the handle, pressed against the hatch. It won't open," says Namu.

They push and heave, fiddle with the lever—and nearly break it.

Maé rolls her eyes and begins to shudder in a chant:

Inasa bwira

Nada ina

Namulongo gazes inwards, sways in a chant:

Maga kasi
Osi osi.
Their spells don't go anywhere.

"Do you think Aunt Umozi is behind it?"

"Who else? This is bad. We can't be airlocked. The electrolysis machine can only do so much."

"And the engine?"

"The moon, the stars, remember? Always our friends. Without them—"

"Aunt Umozi has imprisoned us."

"Like she has imprisoned Azi. That damned Umozi has thrown peril after peril at us. And now a new obstacle. So straight after the homing—the timing is no coincidence. It means Umozi must be worried that we're winning in our search for Azikiwe."

They look at each other miserably across the dining table in the cooker.

Namulee, Namulee... the sea ghost is floating back and forth in agitation.

Namu jumps in excitement. "Perhaps we're close to Auntie Azi!" She looks at Maé. "Why aren't you happy about this?"

"If Umozi is getting worried, she might do worse harm to Azi."

"Maybe my familiar can help."

"You mean the tilapia? You don't know it's your familiar."

True, thinks Namu in misery. The way the fish moves fast in the water, blowing bubbles, all chatty, clicking and whistling, it's probably forgotten its identity and believes it's a playful dolphin.

Shackery-in-a-cabin!

They gaze in astonishment at Phoena's new words.

Shackery-in-a-cabin!

She's dancing on the table in a funny hop, repeating the words in a bad voice from the roof of her mouth. *Shackery-in-a-cabin.* It's as if she's choking.

"This couldn't possibly get worse," says Maé, just as the lights flicker, dim and black out.

The generator groans its last. Now Maé and Namu peer at each other in candlelight.

"We can't run a vessel on spells," says Maé.

"Or find Auntie Azikiwe either."

Shackery-in-a-cabin!

"And that stupid bird with its stupid voice won't stop." Maé glares at Phoena.

"It's not a bird."

"Don't you think I know it?" Maé throws her hands in exasperation.

Shackery-in-a-cabin!

Phoena begins to stretch and stretch and stretch.

Namulee, Namulee... the sea ghost's cry.

"What's happ—" begins Namu.

Maé tackles Namu to the ground away from the phoenix, screams as she burns together with the phoenix that scorches itself in a bright flame of regeneration.

Phoena stands anew in red-gold plumage that reminds Namu of—

"Three words," whispers Maé. "Perfect. Beautiful. Paradise."

Lights inside *Submerse* blink awake and in a dazzle. The whole vessel is lit like heaven.

Phoena opens her mouth and doesn't *kraa-kra*, or *shackery-in-a-cabin!* Her song is a fugue of deep and terrible sadness. She sings in staccato of captivity, a city in the sun, and the edge of darkness.

"The sight of you... is a good reason to sing," says Maé. She tries to rise, weakly. Her whole back is naked. Her thermals have melted and joined with skin. She smells of roasted meat. "I just don't know... why you'd choose such... melancholy."

Namulee, Namulee...

Maé collapses into the sea ghost's welcoming fog.

Who knows the edge of darkness, how or when you might reach it? Is it first light, and then blackness, falling in a pit full of serpents that stare intently at you, flickering tongues before they strike? Is it an abyss that goes and goes deeper inside a bottom that is bottomless, and it's the belly of a basilisk or a carnivorous eel, or the drowning waters of a beastly crocodile trapping you in a killing grip? Is it a feeling like you're on fire, and excruciatingly so, and you're parched and starved and gobbled in gloom? And your spirit is lonesome, your memory smoggy, and your tomorrow smothered for breath?

A sea ghost asks this.

Command the Vessel

Bibi's fog helps with the healing. Namulongo can only guess at treating the burns. First, she cools Maé with a wet compress. It soothes the blisters. She keeps them moist, changing the plant dressing every now and then with a potion of aloe vera, sunflower oil and honey to reduce crust formation.

"Can't I break the blisters?"

"Don't," whispers Maé. Her face is scarred along the cheek that was nearest to the flames. "It'll bring infection." Maé forbids Namu from using a spell. "A phoenix has its own powers..." she explains. "Gods forbid if you mixed those with incantation."

"It's me who took Phoena in—I feel bad."

"No. It's my fault..." says Maé.

Phoena must feel more guilty. The moroseness in her lilted song makes Namu wish for *kraa-kra*, or *shackery-in-a-cabin*! She doesn't tell Maé this. She doesn't tell her mother about Phoena's second regeneration either, how she burned up and rebirthed to a bigger and more perfect self, more red and gold plumage, but sing-wailing a melancholier composition that stopped the moon from shining.

About that... the hatch is fixed, now opening to the surface.

Namu finishes putting on a new skin dressing of crushed aloe in banana leaves. "Maybe we shouldn't be flogging ourselves," she says quietly. "There's not much merit in it."

"I took a beat too long, though I knew the phoenix was transforming, and what happens when it does."

"You're a poor patient at best. It's hell when you moan."

"Sleeping all the time on my belly. Kill me already. Where is the quality of life?"

"I can turn you on your side. It's healed properly."

"No."

"Accept when you need help," Namu says firmly. She puts a calabash to Maé's mouth. "Drink this."

"Is it poison?"

"It's green tea and black pepper. It will cut the swelling."

"Now you're a herbalist?"

"What you need next is wild lettuce tea that will put you to sleep. Because I can't tolerate you. Now take a nap."

"You take a nap."

Namu busies herself with chores. She inspects the hull, angles the periscope, scrapes scum off the shower and checks the oxygen chamber.

Phoena is crooning a pitiful melody. It's a song that's a fugue of breaking glass. It seems to be about flowers—how they wink when you're not looking. How their snow-white petals are suspicious about ebony cats but adore spectral monsters especially those that creep when you turn your back. How conspirators visit your nightmares and morning news, all undrawn to scale.

Namu compacts the trash and ejects it from the watertight exit in the hull. She forces away the urge to paint, because the tough steel of *Submerse* is good as new since Phoena's transformation restored the lights. The engine, the fins, the propellers are all running to perfection. What's interesting is Tila—Namu has named the so-called familiar— always in the eye of the periscope.

Namu wants Maé to get better, but today she's running a temperature. Namu is fatigued and sore from lying on the cold steel floor. But she pushes herself onwards making fish soups for her patient. It's almost contradictory, somewhat carnivorous, that she would have a tilapia for a familiar, but still prepare fish. She makes stock of the baby bluefin, curries the cod, steams the flounder, crushes the bass into a pottage, stir-fries the halibut.

She tends to the bees, brings new flowers for a fresh batch of pollen and spiced honey. She cultivates the veggie patch, prunes the shona cabbage, shakes out the amaranth seeds. She crushes them and bakes bread. She's exhausted! But makes a pickle. Takes octopus from freezer bags in the reefer—residues of the sweeper's last harvest eons ago—Namu no longer harvests fish. Chops the octopus into a tiny pot, adds salt, water, chilli, oregano and sunflower oil, and seals the jar.

The aroma of the rising bread silences Phoena's glum singing and brings her to the cooker. Namu makes a sauce of red eggplant—it's bigger, more crimson than a tomato, and cooks well in a stew. They wash it down with baobab juice.

Maé is worse. "Let me close my eyes just a moment," she whispers, when Namu tries to feed her cowpea gruel.

"I don't want to do it alone," Namu finally breaks. Her voice wobbles. A lone tear trails her cheeks.

Maé tries to smile encouragement. Her once even face is gaunt, ashen. "I must rest, build my strength."

"I can't do it..."

"Yes... you can." Maé puts her fingers on the back of Namu's hand. "*Submerse* is yours now." She smiles again weakly. "You'll succeed."

"I need you, Maé."

"Take us to Azikiwe. She needs us."

"But Maé—"

"This is your go, child. Stop hesitating." Her eyes twinkle in a hint of mischief. "You'll be fine. You and that curselet Phoena, and that tilapia familiar of yours."

She closes her eyes to the blanket of Bibi's fog.

Even a Fish Makes a Difference

Maé scrunches her face, pushes away the bowl. "So bitter. You burnt the cabbage."

"I didn't."

"Then you're determined to poison me."

"Earlier, didn't you want to die, Maé?"

"Nonsense. And what's Phoena doing here? Too bright." She looks at the phoenix. "You don't belong here. Go to the city of the sun or the edge of darkness you've been mauling us with in song."

"That's just mean, Maé. Leave Phoena alone."

"Maybe I should get up." She starts to rise.

"You'll do no such thing." Namu pushes her back into the bunk. "Keep up the ungratefulness and I'll embody you with a spell that will sleep you for eons."

"With both of us eternally sleeping, who'll rescue Azi?"

"Then I'll summon paralymus and abandon you for eons."

Maé succumbs. "Why use a spell of battle when we're not even fighting? Besides, the effects of a paralymus spell are only temporary."

"Before I'm done with you, it'll feel like eons. Now shut up, woman, and sleep."

"Eee, pampula. No. Stop racing ahead of yourself. I gave you command of the vessel, not of my body."

Namu grinds more amaranth seeds and is baking muffins when her mother wanders into the cooker.

"Looks like you're out of trouble, Maé."

"What's happening?"

"I take it you're not asking about the muffins." Namu takes her mother's hand, guides her to the tower. "We've been moving everywhere, reaching nowhere. But now we have a compass."

"And it is?"

"Come, look through the periscope."

Maé looks. "I see a fish."

"*That's* the compass."

"Is that your plan: follow the tilapia?"

"It's no ordinary fish. Tila has been beckoning me to follow and, finally, I listened."

"I hope something more solid than a fish guided your decision on a journey that not only affects us, but Azi's fate."

"Didn't you say even a fish makes a difference?"

"I am turning this vessel."

"And Phoena, Phoena! What have you noticed?"

"I'll avoid the phoenix at all costs."

"Once we started steering towards Tila, Phoena stopped singing those deep and terribly sad songs."

"So she's your familiar too?"

"You're annoyed with me."

"Let me think about that for a short time and I'll confirm with you just how enraged I am by your foolishness."

A Child, Unlearned

"What's that?" Namu points.

"It's a beach," says Maé.

It's as if someone has made a deal with the gods of weather. Though it's night, outside is bright and white. Namu blinks. If this is the edge of darkness, she honestly doesn't mind it.

"It's land," she cries. "Land!"

"I feel foolish for letting you convince me to follow the tilapia."

"And the phoenix. We knew the journey was wrong every time Phoena went maudlin in song, and we changed steer."

A mud-coloured guillemot peers low with its white face, lets out a high-pitched pipe call.

Namulee, Namulee... the sea ghost's animated cry.

"Can't you see, Maé? Phoena and Tila have led us to Auntie Azikiwe. Aunt Umozi must have hidden her here, where we'd never think to search."

"I don't know—"

"Look at Tila, summersaulting in glee. Auntie's here. She must, oh, please, she must be here."

"Is it possible?" whispers Maé.

Staccato piping, then a tremulous whistle from the guillemot.

Phoena begins to stretch. But rather than explode in a new scorcher, then a paradise of plumage, she flies out from the tower in a dazzle of beauty. Her hair cascades in the colour of the sun. Her trail of shimmer sweeps the skies.

Namu cups her hand and calls out from the tower. "Come with?"

"Where did you learn to speak like that?" She looks at the beach. "*Submerse* will have to wait here. Think you can swim out there?"

"Let's, quick Maé."

Namu drags out from the flow and ebb of the tide and onto land. Her phoenix is in a glow overhead. Namu looks backwards. The vessel that is her house disappears behind the ocean. The water wears the pale blue of a pearl she's never seen. A beach dazzles with glistening sand. She sprints to catch up with Maé. Trees of a velvet green remind her of eating avocados. And are those coconut trees? Or palm trees, floppy ears defending their nuts. Here, the call of birds is louder. Merry whistles, chirpy flutes. One bird is singing a cheery squeaker-ree, squeaker-ree. Perhaps they are seasonal, those flowers on a brush. Coned petals in a flaming orange speak the language of this world.

Maé is walking towards a dilapidated cabin on the beach. A long-legged bird with blue-black feathers and a red beak gingerly prowls the beach, unperturbed by the tourists' presence. It's a kind of bird Namu has never seen.

Namu kicks off her shoes and races barefoot. Sand grains tickle between her toes. She avoids a rock, sprints past a brown man walking his mud-faced dog that's otherwise all white. The dog notices her, the man barely registers her. The dog lopes, ears flat. Its tail wags. It barks and leaps at the bird that takes flight.

The shack is a pitiful array the size of a pit latrine. It's tinier than the facilities on *Submerse*. It's near a three-stone hearth all ashed—someone cooked a meal on it centuries ago. Namu picks a rock and approaches the padlocked hut.

"That won't do. The lock is enchanted."

Maé rolls her eyes and begins to shudder in a chant. Nothing happens.

Namulongo drops the rock. She gazes inwards, sways in a chant. The padlock bangs against the wood. Nothing else happens.

"Auntie Azikiwe, if you're in there help us."

A groan.

"Azi!"

"Auntie!"

"Don't make a meal of it," says a melodious, but weak, voice. "Just save me."

"That's like it," says Maé. "You went quiet too long after our last communications."

"Umozi moved me from my submersible to this horrid cabin. Forgive me that she didn't think it was a good idea to install comms.

Get me out!"

"We must spell together, Auntie," cries Namu.

Maé rolls her eyes and shudders in her chant:

Inasa bwira

Nada ina.

Namulongo gazes inwards, sways in a chant:

Maga kasi

Osi osi.

A hiss from inside the hut:

Rozi tasi

Navi dato.

The padlock snaps, and Auntie Azikiwe falls out of the door, gasping for air.

She coughs. "It was a coffin in there! I was better in the submersible before that fool snatched me."

"You survived Umozi."

"I barely scraped through." Delicate reed, musical notes in her voice. "When she found out we were talking, she brought me to this place without technology. Called it my eternal tomb, that no one would find me. But you did." She casts her green-blue eyes at her rescuers. "Thank you." The fern in her green hair is not bouncy on her shoulders. It's parched. Her skin that looked yellow from their control chamber is here a smooth caramel.

"Your eyes—innocent, big and curious—just as I knew," Auntie Azikiwe says. "Don't stare at me, chile, like you're witnessing a ghost."

She's lean and lanky, a sinewy frame, famished a long time. Yet she wears a sweet smell of passionfruit or melon as she envelops Namu in her arms.

"You've got a smell on you, girl."

"There's a story," laughs Maé.

"The smell is jungle," says Namu. "Now I can be a land voyager."

"And a water voyager," says Auntie Azikiwe. "You belong to land and sea. Or land and sea belong to you." She straightens and studies Maé. "You look... business."

"I am."

"Is that unusual?"

"Very. You look... trouble."

"Oh, I feel worse. But maybe look better than you." Auntie Azikiwe touches the scarring along Maé's cheek. "What happened?"

"Your homing spell."

They laugh, embrace.

Namulongo looks at them: Maé's even face, Auntie Azikiwe's high cheek-boned one. She feels overwhelmed. Now that it's happened, she's struggling to accept they're finally together. It's almost a dream, one too good to indulge.

"Now what's this about burns and homing spells?"

"That phoenix you sent. Up, there she is."

"Her name is Phoena," says Namulongo.

"A phoenix? I thought you tried to cook the tilapia, and it bested you."

"I did no such thing. Why would I want to cook a familiar?"

"A familiar? The tilapia is the homing spell."

"What?" cry Namu and Maé in unison. They look upwards at the phoenix.

Namulongo recalls what Maé said about being gifted with fire. It isn't a fire dragon.

"My guess, chile," says Auntie Azikiwe, kneeling to face level, "is that Phoena is the familiar you've so badly been waiting for." She looks at Maé. "Now one or both of you—do something. I'm hungry enough to eat a school of wolf-fish."

"Namulongo can do it."

"Can she, really?"

Namu stretches a hand, fells two coconuts with a chant. They topple in turn, and land at her feet.

"You might still need those toes," says Maé.

These coconuts are giant, compared to the miniature ones Namulongo knows.

"You have a good core, the way you belt out that chant," says Auntie Azikiwe.

Namu pulls the fibre from the kernel, cracks the shell with a rock. "It's a fresh young one. Take it, Auntie. To the richness of the ocean."

"And the strength of belief," whispers Auntie Azikiwe.

She drinks the coconut water in hungry swallows as Maé prepares the second nut. Auntie Azikiwe holds out the nut to Namu. "For you now."

"You drink it."

"Chile."

Namu tastes the sweet and sour nut in the translucent coconut water. She uses her finger to scoop the soft white gelatine. "Here, Auntie."

The second coconut is older, its white meat crunchier. But its aroma is sweeter, and munching its white flesh gives creamier milk.

"I needed this. What I could do with more is some soft stone to chew." Auntie Azikiwe pats her swelling belly. "Maybe you can magic it."

Maé's look has changed.

"Say it," says Auntie Azikiwe. "It's loud in your silence, that thing you say about the spell of creation—how it's forbidden."

"There's obligation," says Maé in a kind voice. "I'm not angry, Azi. Just thankful."

"You always put your own spin on matters." She pats her belly. "You understand it'll be a child, unlearned?"

"Of course."

Denouement

"What's your prognosis?" They are sitting around a hearth fire, the three of them together with Bibi and Phoena. The fire is more for sentiment than a need for light or warmth. Auntie Azikiwe looks at Namulongo, then Maé.

"The early signs are good," says Maé. "What more would anyone want? The child can guide a spell beautifully and smother a kraken."

"Amazing."

"She responds to instruction or reprimand as quickly as you can say it."

"Really?"

"No."

"I'm right here, you know," says Namu.

"It's good to see that you and your mother are getting along," says Auntie Azikiwe.

"Oh, we're feeling each other along the edges," says Maé.

"I see. Protective as ever, clucky. What's that saying about a mother hen?"

"Mother hen, nothing." Maé rises. "Are we rescuing you, or not?"

"No need to make a crowd of it."

"A crowd, or an audience?"

"And the difference?" says Auntie Azikiwe. She looks at Maé, who doesn't answer. "I thought so."

Laughter in the horizon cuts off Maé's reply. The laughter is dissonant, always wrong.

"Looks like Umozi is finally here," says Auntie Azikiwe. "I told you she was using me as bait."

"And she can fly," says Namulongo in wonderment. "Like an evil lightning bird."

"She's mightier than ever, but will never rest until she takes our power or destroys us all," says Maé.

A terrible howl fills Namu with misgiving, fear and dread. The sound is worse in the open than it was on the screen. A face flickers in and out of the sky. But what comes out of the most blackened clouds are not crimson lips, and a gnash of teeth: it's a coffee-skinned woman with a petite petal mouth.

"She's very deceptive," says Auntie Azikiwe. "Be careful.

Together, they watch the descent. Umozi floats to her feet. She has satin skin and golden-brown eyes. Her smooth face, the shape of an egg, is framed in a blue-black fringe, and a sweep of long, slippery hair roped in braids.

Wearing such a kindly face, Aunt Umozi looks like a magus that Namu—if she didn't know different—might want to acquaint with.

Auntie Azikiwe touches Namu's chin. She looks into her eyes. "You have a big role, chile. You understand this?"

Namu nods.

"She runs and flies," says Maé impatiently. "Of course, she understands."

"I have belief," says Namu.

"And courage?" asks Auntie Azikiwe.

"Courage also."

"Good."

"To be clear, I'll dishearten you both with a reminder," says Maé. "A quadity is never five. One of us will die today—"

"And I know just who. She needs to give me back the submersible and my damn whale!" says Auntie Azikiwe.

"... and if you care about that baby—" Maé looks at the sky, "maybe it's better that you don't fight."

"The baby is kicking for battle."

"In which case, it had better know how to spell."

Auntie Azikiwe's glance at Maé is quizzical. "I've never known you to give in that easy."

Maé shrugs. "There's a lot on the line," she says. "And I've never known myself to shy from help."

"Then let's see who gets first hands on evil."

"First, I'd better tell this one something." Maé looks at Namulongo. "That out there is evil. Don't just run at it."

No-one laughs, the tension taut. A big wind swirls around their poses: heads tilted, knees bent, palms attentive to spelling. Phoena swoops down in a blaze, and joins them. Her ruby eyes are fierce. Bibi's fog is full of menace.

Umozi walks towards them in a graceful flow. She breaks into a sprint in a stream of braids. Her soft brown eyes are kinder than ever.

"Don't forget just how potent she is," hisses Auntie Azikiwe.

Maé rolls her eyes and begins to shudder in a chant.

Namulongo gazes inwards, sways in a chant.

Auntie Azikiwe glares, hisses her chant.

A trio of spells falls out in unison, in a language of Babel:

Inasa bwira
Nada ina.

~

Maga kasi
Osi osi.

~

Rozi tasi
Navi dato.

A whirling hurricane gulps the four magi into the gut of a fierce battle.

Acknowledgements

"Sita and the Fledgling" first published in *Fantasy on Four Feet* by Black Ink, March 2022

"Nyamizi, the Skinless One" first published in *Sorghum & Spear: The Way of Silk and Stone* by SUBSUME and Outland Entertainment, May 2022.

Also by Eugen Bacon

Fiction

Chasing Whispers
Mage of Fools
Saving Shadows
Danged Black Thing
Speculate (with Dominique Hecq)
The Road to Woop Woop & Other Stories
Ivory's Story
Black Moon: Graphic Speculative Flash Fiction
Hadithi & The State of Black Speculative Fiction (with Milton Davis)
It's Folking Political
Her Bitch Dress
Claiming T-Mo

Non-Fiction

An Earnest Blackness
Writing Speculative Fiction

About the Author

EUGEN BACON is an African Australian author of several novels and fiction collections as well as *Writing Speculative Fiction* by Bloomsbury. Her books *Ivory's Story*, *Danged Black Thing*, and *Saving Shadows* were finalists for the British Science Fiction Association Awards, and she has been nominated for, or has won awards including the Foreword Indies Award, Bridport Prize, Copyright Agency Prize, Horror Writers Association Diversity Grant, Otherwise Fellowship, Nommo Award, and others. Bacon's creative work has appeared in *Award Winning Australian Writing*, *Fantasy Magazine*, *Year's Best African Speculative Fiction*, and *Fantasy & Science Fiction*. Visit her website at eugenbacon.com

9 781947 879447